Christine P........................
all her life ....
when she w........................
published her first book w........................
Josephine. Christine has writt........................
translated into eleven languages. She is ....
pony books but has also written the very successful Jessie
series about a dog and general fiction stories for younger
readers.

Christine has four children and lives with her husband,
Julian Popescu, in a moated Parsonage in Suffolk with two
horses, a dog and a cat.

Other Pony Books by Christine Pullein-Thompson

Published by Cavalier Paperbacks

A Pony In Distress

I Rode A Winner

The Lost Pony

For Want of A Saddle

Stolen Ponies

HORSEHAVEN

Christine Pullein-Thompson

CAVALIER PAPERBACKS

This revised edition published by Cavalier Paperbacks
1999
Burnham House
Jarvis St
Upavon
Wilts SN9 6DU

The right of Christine Pullein-Thompson to be identified
as the author of this work has been asserted by her in
accordance with the Copyright, Designs and Patents Act
1988

Cover illustration by Mark Smallman

ISBN 1-899470-13-1

Printed and bound in Great Britain by Cox & Wyman,
Reading, Berks

CHAPTER ONE

A TERRIBLE YEAR AT WOODSIDE

I couldn't speak. I looked round the bungalow which was always in chaos, and which I loved. I thought, I'll never stand in the yard and smell horse again, never arrive first in the morning and see welcoming heads looking over loose-box doors, softly nickering. It's over, I thought, and I'll have nowhere to go any more. I saw myself at home arguing with my mother in the kitchen, felt the smallness of it, saw Dad sitting unemployed in the living room, his hands helpless on his knees. I saw myself staying in bed all day; the sunlight on the flowered curtains in my room, the sound of traffic going by, and nothing to look forward to ever again.

"You can't do it Jenny. I won't let you. There must be a way out," I yelled like a wounded animal in pain. "And what about your rescued animals? What about Squid and Fidget? You can't just sell them, you can't." And now Jenny was crying too, for a moment we clung to each other; then I rushed outside into the darkening twilight unable to bear another minute in her house.

"There's no hay. I've no more money. Can't you understand?" Jenny called after me. "I'll be taken up for cruelty to animals if I go on the way I'm going. The bank won't let me have any more money; I've got to sell up. There's no other way."

"There must be," I shouted, looking for my bike, my head numb with despair, my hands shaking with shock. The front light did not work. I didn't care. I didn't mind what happened to me at that moment. Woodside was to be sold, the place I loved best in all the world. It was going under the hammer in a week's time. A week, I had just a week to save Woodside.

"Take care. You haven't got a light," called Jenny. "Wait a minute." But I didn't want to wait. I wanted to lie on my bed and cry. I wanted to think alone with the door shut. As I rode my bike home I imagined houses rising where horses had once grazed. Close after Close of them - Stable Close, Field Close, Horseman's Close. The grass would go. There would be cul-de-sac after cul-de-sac. Street lights, pavements. Only the wood would remain, the wood which had given the stables their name, carpeted in bluebells in the spring, deep in orange and gold leaves in the autumn; the beech trees tall and bare in winter, reaching high into the sky glistening with frost, tinselled with snow. The wood would stay because it had a conservation order on it, but it would change; the bluebells would be wrenched from the earth by rapacious hands, to wilt and die in vases, trampled paths would appear, fires would be lit scorching the trunks of trees, residents of the Closes would dump their rubbish there; soon it would resemble a weary, disheartened town wood and the magic would be gone for ever.

"What's the matter love?" I was home now, but I hadn't seen the journey or felt it - I had been on automatic pilot all the way. My mother was putting scones on to a plate.

"Nothing, nothing," I shouted.

"Where are you going?"

"Upstairs, can't you see?" I asked.

"What about something to eat?"

"No thank you." I shut my bedroom door, lay on my bed. I thought, I can't stay here day after day; for I had no friends. I hadn't needed them until now. Woodside had been enough. Without it, I would be lost. My mother had said once, "I don't know what you'll do if that place shuts down. Don't you want anything else? Don't you want a social life, Cath?" I hated being Cath. I was Cathy at Woodside. And I had friends of a kind there - Josh and all the other helpers, but most of all Jenny. And of course the horses, who never made unkind remarks about clothes or spots on your face; who were always the same, even if you were late feeding or breakfast wasn't up to scratch. And they were all different too. People think animals of a kind are all the same, but it isn't true; they all have their own characteristics, and they all respond to kindness, or nearly all.

My mother called up the stairs: "Do you want me to bring you some tea?"

"No," I yelled. "I tell you I'm all right. I don't need

anything," and I nearly added, "not ever again."

Later I went downstairs, took a coin out of my mother's handbag, and went out slamming the front door after me. Our telephone had been taken away, but the kiosk was only fifty yards along the road. This evening there was no one in it. I knew Josh's number by heart. Have I told you about Josh? He was fourteen then, a year older than me. His mother was a nurse, his father a Swede who worked for a charity (OXFAM or Children in Need or something similar) and was away a lot. Josh had his father's fair hair, his hazel eyes, shaded by pale lashes. But he had his mother's neat hands and rather large mouth.

I dialled his number. Suddenly I was very cold. As I waited I prayed that the ansaphone would not be on. It wasn't. Josh answered. "It's Cathy. It's urgent. Can you ring me back?" I asked, and gave him the number of the phone box. People were entering the pub just down the road. Loud voices cursed the government. Someone laughed. The phone rang. I picked it up.

"Where are you?" Josh asked.

"Not at home. I'm in a call box because our telephone has been taken. I'm all right Josh, it's Woodside," my voice would hardly say Woodside, so profound was my despair. "It's going to shut down. Jenny's selling up."

There was a silence before Josh asked, "But why?"

"No money of course. It's the government," I said. At that time everyone was blaming the government for everything. If our house had burnt down my parents would have blamed the government. It had become the biggest scapegoat in history.

"You mean the business rate?" asked Josh. "But we can't let it happen. We must do something."

"I know." I was starting to cry again. "It will go for houses, disappear for ever. And what will we do then?" I cried.

"It's worse for Jenny, it's her life," Josh said.

"It's my life too." I was holding the receiver so tightly now that my hand had stuck to it. I was holding it as though it was a lifeline, as though I would drown if I let go.

Like many others, we had both learnt to ride at Woodside, myself in return for helping (and I wasn't the only one who had learnt that way). Of course the recession had made the numbers of pupils dwindle; we all knew that. But that wasn't the only problem; there were the horses at livery, whose owners only paid when they could afford to; there were the horses and ponies soft-hearted Jenny had rescued who were not fit to do a day's work - Fidget and Squid, dear patient Trooper, and Fantasy. There were the vets' bills and the hay bills and the farrier's bills. Worse than that the tack room had been broken into twice and everything taken. It had been a terrible year at Woodside. Inwardly, as I stood in the telephone ki-osk on that cold October evening, I was hating my parents for not being rich enough to help, for not even having the money to pay for our telephone to be re-connected. I imagined them rich. I imagined my father saying, "I'll help with a few thou." But life wasn't like that I thought, and no one was going to help.

Josh was still talking. "Are you there?" he asked.

"Yes, of course I am."

"Oh great, I thought for a moment that you had fainted," he said.

"I'm not that feeble," I answered.

"But it's going to hit you worse than anyone else Cathy. I mean it's been like a sanctuary to you, hasn't it?" Josh continued.

And suddenly the word 'Sanctuary' seemed to float in the air, and I kept thinking 'Sanctuary,' what exactly does it mean and why is it suddenly so important? And then I knew. And now I wasn't cold any more. I was shouting into the receiver, "Sanctuary Josh, you've said it, we'll turn Woodside into a Sanctuary, a place for rescued horses and ponies, a refuge. What do you think? It's possible isn't it Josh? It can be done, can't it?"

There was a short terrifying silence while I thought, if I can't convince Josh, I'll never convince Jenny, and then he said, "perhaps we should sleep on it."

And I shouted then, "We can't, there isn't time. She's having the place auctioned in a week. We must decide now. Is it on? Is it possible?" And now in my mind I saw animals arriving, emaciated horses, mares in foal, blind horses, battered ponies, tired humble donkeys. I was burning up with excitement; and suddenly it seemed the most important moment of my entire life.

"It will have to be a charity," said Josh slowly.

"Of course," I shouted. "We can sell Christmas cards, have car boot sales, sponsored walks, flag days, the whole lot. What do you think?"

"I think it's terrific. But why didn't Jenny tell me she was closing down, why did she only tell you?" And

I knew by his voice that he was jealous , that he hadn't wanted to hear it second-hand from me.

"You weren't there at the right moment, I was," I said. "Life is like that, isn't it? Dad says you have to be in the right place at the right time," I added before I replaced the receiver, and ran home on legs crazy with hope. "I took some money from your purse," I told my mother.

"I know," she said. "It doesn't matter. You are smiling now, that's what matters."

I ate chips without any fish because we could only afford the chips. I ate them with my fingers. And I didn't taste a thing. I put my arms around my mother and said, "Thank you."

"What for? What's happened?" she asked.

"Just an idea, just a wonderful, wonderful idea. Can you lend me some money? I'm going to phone Jenny," I said. "It's urgent. I must hurry, because time is running out."

There was a man in the kiosk this time. He kept putting more and more money into the coin box. A biting wind blew leaves along the pavement. I grew cold waiting and my enthusiasm started to drain away. But when at last I rang Jenny's number there was no answer. Where had she gone? Was she already discussing the sale of Woodside, not waiting for the auction, I wondered? I dialled again and again until a large woman standing outside called, "Are you going to be there all night darling? Isn't he in then?"

"It isn't a him," I answered replacing the receiver. If my bike's lights had been working, I would have ridden to Woodside then, but the night was dark now,

11

and the road full of cars.

That night I dreamt that Woodside was in flames. Jenny stood in the yard laughing, while I fought to rescue the poor frantic horses still trapped in their loose-boxes. Then Josh appeared shouting, "We're too late. It's all over for ever and ever. But never mind, they'll all go to heaven." I woke in a sweat. Outside the street lamps were still on.

CHAPTER TWO

"I CAN'T AFFORD TO KEEP
ANOTHER ONE"

The street lights were still on when I set out for
Woodside the next morning. I stood on the pedals of
my bike. I was afraid Jenny would turn down my idea.
I was afraid I was already too late. The horses welcomed me - grey Trooper, long backed Fantasy. The
horses at Livery - Mrs Sykes' bay Romance, Barney
Bank's two greys; and in the field behind the stables
Roy Redman's polo ponies were watching me too as
though I carried heaven on my back. While in the
bottom field Squid and Fidget were also waiting, ears
pricked, small eyes shining. The riding school had
closed weeks ago. Jenny had hoped the liveries would
help her to survive without lessons, but with four rescued horses eating their heads off and bad debts, they
hadn't. So three weeks ago she had sold five horses
including my favourite pony Twilight. I had tried not

to mind too much, but watching Twilight go still haunted me. My mother wanted me to get a job then, any job, but there weren't any. Now carrying buckets of feed, I was praying I could spend the rest of my life at Woodside. The stabled horses had feeds; the amount for each was written on a blackboard in the tack room; the quantity had dwindled recently and when I loaded a whole bale of hay on to a wheelbarrow to take to the polo ponies, Jenny opened a window and called, "Not so much, take some off Cathy, we've hardly any left."

She was still in her dressing gown. I guessed that she too had had a sleepless night because it can't be pleasant to watch your life crumbling before your eyes. Then she called, "When you've finished, come inside, the kettle's on."

I thought, in a few days she may not be saying that ever again. The stables will be padlocked, the horses gone. It didn't bear thinking about.

A few minutes later Josh appeared leading a chestnut horse and I saw straightaway that he was a very sick horse. "I think he's dying. I couldn't leave him where he was to die alone," Josh said brushing tears from his eyes.

The horse had three white socks, a bedraggled flaxen mane and tail and he was soaked in sweat and shivering. We put him in a loose box, before Jenny rushed from the house crying, "Oh no, not another one! Oh how could you Josh? How could you? And what will Mark say?" (Mark is Jenny's unhorsey partner. Josh calls him 'The Devil's Advocate', whatever that means).

"I couldn't pass on the other side. His paddock is full

14

of ragwort and there was nothing else for him to eat,"
Josh said now looking guilty.

"I can't afford to keep another horse. They've all got
to go. Can't you understand?" demanded Jenny.

"Have you told her about your idea Cathy?" Josh
asked filling a bucket with water at the yard tap.

"Not yet."

"Well get on with it then," he said.

I was so afraid that Jenny would say no to a Sanctuary that I was scared to speak and afraid to face myself afterwards if she turned it down.

"I think this could be a Horse Sanctuary, a refuge, a
charity. I think we could raise money for the rescued
horses here. Other people do it all the time," I said at
last, as though there was a Horse Sanctuary at every
street corner.

Jenny stared at me before exclaiming, "But think of
the work Cathy!"

"We will do the work," replied Josh finding a rug for
the chestnut horse. "We'll raise the money too."

"With boot sales, and raffles, and lots of other events,"
I added. "It'll be fun."

"But we need £500 straight away," replied Jenny.

"We'll find it," said Josh. "I'll sell my computer for
starters."

Jenny said then that she would have to think about
it. Josh said that we would rehome the rescued horses
when they were fit again. He said it could be an ongo-
ing concern. Josh is the most persuasive person I
know. He made everything sound dead easy - no more
rates to pay, no more grumbling owners, refusing to
pay what they owed. All we would have to do was to

15

raise money. Josh made it sound like a picnic in the summer, as he followed Jenny talking, persuading, countering every doubt she raised. But I knew it wouldn't be like that. I knew it would be a hard grind all the way, but satisfying too. It would give us all a real purpose in life. I saw the fourteen loose-boxes full of patients, cross embittered Mrs Sykes removing Romance to a smarter establishment; the polo ponies going away to play polo; only Barney Banks' horses remaining. And perhaps if the charity became very rich it might take me on as a paid worker, part time of course.

We sat in the kitchen drinking coffee and now the sun was shining outside.

"You'll never sell this place, not at the moment; you know that Jenny don't you, because nothing is selling at the moment, absolutely nothing," said Josh emphatically.

We drank coffee out of thick mugs. "I'll look into it," said Jenny.

"But I have. I know about charities, my father works for one. I can get hold of all the know-how we'll ever need. I tell you it's dead easy Jenny," Josh continued. "Dead easy."

Jenny was wavering now.

"We'll hold a boot sale the week after next, surely the bank can wait till then," I said.

"And you can cancel the auction," added Josh smoothly. "And I'll advertise my computer in tomorrow's Evening Echo and I know Mum will lend me £100 if we need it," he finished.

"And once we're established we can have Open Days

like other sanctuaries; and sell things," I added.

"We can make the Pony Club pay to come here."

"We can run a Horse Show." Suddenly the 'could' had become 'can'.

"I think I had better see my bank manager," said Jenny.

"Do you want me to come with you?" asked Josh. "My uncle is one, so I understand bank managers."

But Jenny declined the offer.

CHAPTER THREE

POOR JACK

When all the horses had been fed and watered, the mucking out done, and Jenny had gone to see her bank manager, Josh told me how he had found the chestnut horse with the flaxen mane and tail. "He had got out of his field and was standing by this plush garage," he said. "And he looked awful. Fortunately the gates weren't locked and I went in and felt his ears and they were absolutely freezing so I knew he must be ill. I rang the front door bell for ages and rattled the letterbox, but nothing happened. I even looked through the windows and called, "Anyone at home?" Then I peered through a window into the garage and saw it was empty. After that I went to the paddock and it was full of droppings and dying ragwort, and not a bit of hay anywhere and then of course I knew why he was ill - he had eaten the ragwort. You can guess how I felt then Cathy, really sick."

I nodded. I could picture it all. I knew the house, which was new with a swimming pool attached.

"And so I put my belt round his neck and led him

here. It was a bit short but we managed. But he's on his last legs, he can hardly stagger. I could kill his owners. Why do people buy horses if they don't want to look after them?" finished Josh.

"As status symbols," I answered.

We looked at the chestnut horse. In spite of the rug he was still shivering, and the mash Jenny had given him was uneaten.

"Don't we need the vet?" I asked.

"Jenny's trying to contact the owners first. But yes, I think we do," said Josh. "It's just that Jenny owes them lots of money already."

"Oh, how I hate money," I said.

Seconds later Jenny returned. "Thumbs up. I think the bank is sympathetic. The manager has a horse himself, which helps," she said.

"What about our new inmate? Don't we need the vet?" asked Josh.

"Yes definitely. I went to the police, but they know nothing and I stopped at the house and there was no one there," said Jenny. "The owners are called Freemantle."

"I'm going to ring the vet if you won't, Jenny," said Josh. "His owners will pay, we'll make them. We'll find out their name and then prosecute for cruelty." Josh's face was turning red; I had never seen him so angry before. I looked at the sick horse again while they went indoors, and I knew with awful certainty that he was going to die.

Then I started to imagine the stables as a refuge, with every loose-box full. I wondered what Jenny's partner Mark would say when he saw the new horse, for it was Mark who wanted to balance the books, who hated living in the shadow of debt.

A few minutes later Josh said, "A vet's on his way. It's too late of course; but at least we'll have tried."

"What about the bank manager?" Is this place going to be a refuge? I must know," I asked next.

"I'm dithering. I must speak to Mark," replied Jenny who had joined us.

"There's nothing else you can do," Josh said. "You can't just shut it down. What about Squid and Fidget?"

"And Fantasy and Trooper?" I added.

"You can't let them down, Jenny. This is their home. You can't take it away from them," said Josh.

Mrs Sykes was rugging up Romance. "I see you've rescued another lame duck," she said.

"But not for long. He's on his way out Mrs S," Josh answered.

"To whom does he belong?"

"We're not absolutely sure yet," I said.

"Not sure?"

"That's right."

Mrs Sykes always wanted to know everything. She was thin with rather a long nose and eyes which squinted especially when she was curious. She wanted us to call her by her Christian name which was Betty, but somehow we couldn't, not even Jenny. She wanted Romance to be a dressage horse and imagined herself reaching Prix St George standard, when Romance had a short stride and a thick neck and she had yet to win a Novice competition. But no one dared to tell her this, for as Josh said, "We all have dreams," (though what his were I had no idea.)

The vet came at last. He was young and friendly. He gave the chestnut horse three injections. I don't think he had even seen a case of ragwort poisoning before.

"It destroys the liver, same as when you drink too much alcohol over a long period," Jenny said. Jenny knew all about ragwort poisoning. As a child she had watched her pony die of it. Jenny knows more about horsey ailments than most vets. "The trouble is you can't repair a liver," she added now. "And please don't send the bill here. Send it to a Mr Freemantle at Field House. He isn't my horse. My helper Josh found him dying."

"All alone," added Josh for good measure.

Later Mark returned from trying to sell a new type of washing machine to shops which had hundreds of similar models already cluttering up their floor space. Nervously Jenny told him about the possibility of Woodside becoming a charity. They went inside together and now my heart was going thump, thump, as fast as an overcharged engine.

"Will he stop her? Can he?" I asked.

"I don't know."

"It's her place. And I thought it was all settled," I said.

"He can still influence her."

"If it was my place, I wouldn't be influenced by anyone," I replied.

"But it isn't your place," said Josh as though he were talking to a moron.

"Has she cancelled the auction?"

"I don't know," said Josh. and now fear was on the agenda again. We looked at the chestnut horse. He was quiet and he wasn't sweating any more.

"He's not in any pain," said Josh.

The horse had drunk a little water. I could see that once he had been beautiful with a large eye, long sloping shoulder and the sort of head which pulls at your heart strings.

"And he must have cost a fair sum. I would like to kill his owners, wring their necks, or give them nothing but ragwort to eat."

"Same here." But even as we spoke a sleek Mercedes with tinted glass glided into the yard. Out of it stepped a man with grey hair and the face of an alert dog wearing glasses.

Looking at us he demanded, "Well and where is the beast?" And then he said, "Do you know who I am - I'm Mr Freemantle, and I've come to take home my daughter's horse."

"Well you are out of luck," replied Josh in an icy voice. "Because your daughter's horse is dying, slowly and horribly if you want to know, and it's your fault."

And now a girl leapt from the car screaming, "Where is he? I want him back. I want him back now, this instant." She ran across the yard screaming, "Jack, Jack. You're all right aren't you? Oh my darling Jack."

"We've had a vet," I said.

"We got entangled in a pile up. We should have got back yesterday. I see the fence is down," said Mr Freemantle quite calmly, as though horses were dying every day of the week.

Jack didn't recognise the girl. He was standing at the back of his box and anyone could see he was dying. The next few minutes were really ghastly. Jenny

22

and Mark emerged from the house and explained what had happened. Next Mark shone a torch in Jack's eyes and said, "He's unconscious, sir."

"What standing up?" inquired Mr Freemantle in an irritated voice.

"Yes, standing up," replied Jenny. "Shall I ring our vet now and have him put down, because I think it's the kindest thing to do. I need your permission first."

But Mr Freemantle insisted that he had to consult his insurance company before anything further was done. He told Samantha to sit in the car and to stop blubbering like a five year old. "I'll buy you another horse, a jumper this time. One which won't eat ragwort, a grey like you've always wanted," he said.

Mr Freemantle talked on his mobile phone. Samantha got out and looked at Jack. She was wearing school uniform - a horrible brown tunic, thick tights, lace-up shoes and a brown blazer with a shield on its pocket.

"Okay," said Mr Freemantle letting go of his telephone. "All in order. Give this card to your vet after the deed is done, get him to fill it up, and make sure he does it properly. The company will take care of everything." He wrote on a card before handing it to Jenny. He sounded as though he had just completed a successful business transaction. "What's left will go for meat of course," he continued. "That's the rule. He was an expensive horse, it's lucky he was insured. And here's my address," he continued, handing Jenny a smaller card. "Let me know what I owe you."

Samantha was still crying and he told her to get in the car and to stop being a wimp. "He was only a horse," he said. "And I'll buy you a better one next week, a real champion this time."

"What a terrible man," exclaimed Jenny.

"I would like to give him nothing to eat for days," I said as they left.

"I would like to force ragwort down his silly throat," said Josh.

I won't dwell on what happened next. Mark dealt with the vet, while the rest of us saw to the other horses, trying to hide our grief. But there was another blow still to come.

Mrs Sykes had gone home. Jenny was unusually quiet, which is often a sign that something unpleasant is afoot. Josh was still muttering about the Freemantles. "They should be prevented from having another horse," he fumed, "and certainly not a grey show jumper. It's diabolical that people as awful as they are can just go out and buy a horse - they're not fit to keep a guinea pig."

The stabled horses were in an awkward mood. They refused to stay still when their rugs were changed, knocked over buckets, while the ones in fields kept imagining disaster on every gust of wind. And though we all knew that it was Jack's death which had upset them, none of us said so.

After the deed was done, Mark went into Jenny's house without speaking. Mark stands five feet ten in his socks and has reddish hair. He is thin-lipped and doesn't laugh easily, nor does he talk much. Sometimes I wonder what he is thinking. Does he mind me and Josh hanging around? Doesn't he want Jenny just to himself? But I have yet to know the answer.

When we had finished settling the horses and Jenny reappeared, Josh said, "How about the Sanctuary? When can we start raising money?"

There was a horrible mind boggling pause while Jenny looked uncomfortable, before she said, "Mark still wants this place to go to auction. It may not reach its reserve for all we know. But it's been widely advertised and we can't suddenly withdraw it."

"Still go to auction?" I shrieked. "But it can't. And why should Mark decide? It's your place Jenny, not his."

"Of course you can cancel an auction, right up to the very last minute, but you don't want to, do you?" cried Josh accusingly.

"It can't go for building, because it's outside the settlement area," continued Jenny as though neither of us had spoken. "So I don't think anyone will buy it."

CHAPTER FOUR

SAMANTHA

Josh and I went to the auction on our bikes. It was a lovely autumn morning, the sort of day when you should be riding through woods, deep in orange leaves, or galloping over a hill, with the smell of horse in your nostrils and joy in your heart. The town centre was full of bustle and noise. We chained our bikes to a rail and hurried into the town hall, a stately grey building with wide steps to it and many tall windows. In the main hall we found more than a hundred people waiting for the auction to begin. Jenny and Mark were sitting together holding hands. Josh and I sat in the back, and already my heart was thumping.

"Don't nod by mistake or you might let yourself in for a lot of expense," said Josh smiling.

I thought it a silly thing to say and I didn't smile back.

A farm was auctioned first with a thousand acres and pig and dairy units. The auctioneer was a large man with a red face and the gift of the gab. He went on and on about the farm, while I wriggled and squirmed with suspense and my heart thumped louder than ever. I felt like shouting, 'Get on with it, will you.' But at last he came to Woodside. He described it as a highly desirable property with many fine features including a large covered school, fourteen loose-boxes, a tack room, hay sheds and thirty acres of well maintained paddocks. "And as well as all this there are five acres of woodland including some valuable timber, and living accommodation which could be enlarged without planning problems." He continued, "So as you have just heard Woodside is a fine property and ideal for equine pursuits."

Spurred on by the auctioneer, the bidding started at £100,000.

Knowing nothing of property prices, £100,000 sounded like a fortune to me. "So Woodside has been sold," I hissed to Josh, standing up, my eyes blinded with tears.

With an embarrassed sigh, Josh pushed me down again. "For goodness sake, they are still bidding," he muttered through clenched teeth.

The bids came slowly; a man in a husky bidding against a woman wearing a fur coat; a young man with a sharp look about him bidding too. The older man looked large and prosperous; the woman looked small and rich. I hated them both instantly. As for the young man I reckoned that he must be bidding for someone else. I imagined the woman building a mansion where Jenny's house now stood. I saw the man fighting the Council for planning permission for houses, wheedling, bullying and bribing and I wanted to run out of the hall and never return. By this time the young man had dropped out.

"Let's go home," I whispered to Josh. "It's going to be sold and there's no hope."

"Do what you like, I'm staying," he said, and I was too shy to stand up and walk out alone. I sat biting my nails instead.

The bidding reached £200,000. I sneaked a look at Jenny and Mark; they were still holding hands. And now the auctioneer was shouting, "I'm bid £200,000, any improvement on £200,000 and I thought that those words will go on in my head for ever. Then he shouted, "Going, going gone," and he banged the table with his gavel saying in a gloomy voice, "Not sold."

"What does he mean, not sold?" I asked Josh, hope beginning to flutter weakly inside me.

"He means just what he said, not sold. It must have had a reserve price on it of at least £250,000," explained Josh standing up.

"So it's over," I said unable to believe our luck.

"Yes, come on, we can celebrate," said Josh smiling. "We can have our Sanctuary now Cathy, you realise that don't you? There's nothing to stop us now because it seems that no one wants to pay a fair price after all. I expect they don't relish the house. It does smell horribly horsey, particularly if the horse rugs are drying near the radiators. And the kitchen is thirty years out of date." But even as he spoke, Josh was laughing, and then I was too, and neither of us could stop. We stumbled down the steps into the street in an undignified way, still laughing.

Jenny and Mark were talking to a man in an anorak

whom Josh said was a journalist, while I was thinking, I'll remember this moment for ever. Mark looked gloomy whereas Jenny turned round to give us a small wave and then the thumbs up sign. Outside it was raining, but our bikes were still there.

"Where to," I cried rubbing tears of laughter from my eyes.

"To Woodside of course," cried Josh.

I don't remember much of our ride there. The bicycles were as boring as usual and I remember yearning for a pair of pricked ears in front of me and the clip clop of hoofs, instead of ugly handlebars and the wet swish of tyres on tarmac.

Once Josh turned round to call, "We'll be able to ride the inmates, test them for new homes," and he was laughing again, neither of us could stop laughing now and our hearts sang with it, and our bikes wobbled. We left the town behind and there were high banks on each side of us now; and we threw down our bikes and picked blackberries and ate them. And now the sky cleared as the clouds swept away like galleons in full sail. And everything looked twice as beautiful, because we were happy.

"I would have gone mad without Woodside," Josh said.

"Same here."

"Mum won't be too pleased. She was hoping for a rest from hay in the soup and mud on the floor," Josh said laughing.

"Dad wants me to have a job, a real one, but what's that?" I asked.

"It doesn't exist any more if you ask me," replied

29

Josh.

And now every time we looked at each other we started laughing and our bikes wobbled more and more until an angry motorist wound down his car window to call, "What's the matter with you? Are you on drugs or something? Or do you think you own the whole damned road?"

"We're just happy," I called back.

"Sorry sir," apologised Josh still laughing.

When we reached Woodside, horses called to us like friends, real friends that is, and there was a lovely smell of horse and hay, and wet earth. And now I was imagining the future again and I wanted to shout to the heavens, "Thank you."

Later press photographers appeared and two helpers called Gillian and Sarah; and we stood with Jenny and Mark smiling until our faces ached, while cameras clicked. Then Jenny turned to us to say, "It's settled; there's no turning back. Our sanctuary will be all over The Evening Echo tomorrow; and I could see that half of her was afraid and half happy.

"You can have my computer on permanent loan. I hate it, and you'll need one," Josh said.

"And I'll be here every spare moment of my life," I promised.

Then Josh told thirteen year old Gillian and nine year old Sarah what had happened and they cried things like "Hurray" and "Great" and "Fantastic!" And the sun was still shining.

Then Mark appeared with some weak cider and an armful of glasses and said, " for better or worse." And then we toasted our sanctuary again and again.

"Mum will organise A boot sale for you. She's great at them," offered Gillian.

"And a jumble sale," added Sarah.

"With a cake stall," added Gillian.

"There's no time to lose," said Jenny.

"We'll have the boot sale here next week then," answered Gillian who has hazel eyes and fair hair to her shoulders. "I'll make some posters tonight."

Then Jenny wanted to know what exactly happened at a boot sale. "You see I've never been to one," she said.

And then of course Gillian and Sarah cried, "Never been to a boot sale? Wow!" Next Gillian explained that people paid money for a pitch and then sold things from the backs of their cars. "Things they don't want mostly," she said.

"Not just boots then?" asked Josh laughing.

"No. They sell things from the boots of their cars. The back part, stupid," said Gillian thumping him. You know what I mean, Josh."

"We'll lobby for sponsorship. Go round the shops," said Josh ignoring Gillian's thumping. "We need a Mr Sainsbury."

"A horsey one. Most millionaires prefer endowing colleges which will go on for ever," replied Jenny.

Jenny gave us sandwiches for lunch. "Don't think this will happen every day," she said.

Then we discussed a name. None of us thought WOODSIDE HORSE SANCTUARY sounded quite right. It was too long for one thing.

"We need something catchy," suggested Mark. "Something easy to remember."

"What about Horse Hospital?" suggested Sarah.

"But it's not going to be a hospital, idiot," said Gillian.

"The Horse Rescue Centre," I suggested.

"Too long," said Josh.

And then of course we started to get silly, to suggest names like WOODSIDE HORSES' HOME FOR THE ELDERLY, and HORSES RETREAT and HAPPY HOME FOR HORSES. And then Jenny cried "I've got it. HORSEHAVEN all in one word. Because it will be a haven for horses and it's short and catchy, isn't it Mark?"

"And easy to spell," I said.

"So our address will be: HORSEHAVEN, WOODSIDE, TREADMILL LANE, COWFORD and then the code. What do you think?" asked Jenny.

"Great," I cried.

"Fantastic," echoed the others.

"Let's make sure it's absolutely right," suggested Mark fetching a dictionary.

While I kept muttering to myself Horsehaven and it sounded the most beautiful name in the world.

Mark read out, "Haven: Refuge, Harbour, Port." And Jenny said, "It's perfect, because in a way it will be all four."

And so it was settled. We talked for a bit longer before we went outside to muck out the loose-boxes which had not been done earlier. The stabled horses were turned out in rugs. When the time came to bring them in, Romance wouldn't be caught. In the end we left him for later, "To stew in his own juice," Jenny said - and went inside and drank tea out of thick mugs and Gillian rang her mother to say that she and Sarah wouldn't be home for another hour at least.

And Josh said, "My mother's hardly ever at home, so I don't have to bother."

"And my parents don't mind as long as they know where I am and of course it's always the same place, ie. here," I said happily.

Then we talked about rehoming the horses and ponies already at Horsehaven. Jenny said that we would have to be very very careful where they went and that we would have an Open Day at Christmas and take it from there.

Josh said that all Fidget and Squid did was to chew the fences, so they must be bored, and that grey Trooper and black Fantasy needed more love.

"But we won't sell them will we?" I asked.

"No, they'll go on loan and we'll inspect them regularly and ask for them back any time we like. It will all be in an agreement," Jenny said.

It was getting dark. Gillian and Sarah disappeared on their bikes. Josh and I took small feeds and a whole bale of hay to the polo ponies. The sun had set all red and gold on the horizon. Birds chirped sleepily in the trees in the home paddock. "Tomorrow the news will have broken. Anything may happen after that," Josh said spreading hay into equal heaps.

"Like what?" I asked.

"Like a huge donation appearing from nowhere," Josh said laughing.

Mum and Dad were not very impressed when I told them about HORSEHAVEN. Mum asked, "Why not a haven for people? There's plenty of them needing one."

Dad said, "Is that what you are going to do when you leave school then - run a horses' home?"

"People have choices, and they aren't chained up for weeks on end, or sold, or trapped in fields dying of hunger. There is a difference Mum, I said. "And Dad, if there aren't any real jobs, what's wrong with looking after horses?" I added before rushing upstairs and sitting on my bed. I thought then, whatever I do, it will never be good enough for my parents. Why can't they say something nice, just for a change?

The next day was Saturday. During the morning Samantha appeared at Woodside. "I've come to say I'm sorry," she told Jenny. "I saw the bit in the local paper and I want to help. I brought you a copy. Look!" And there was the headline: WOODSIDE BECOMES A SANCTUARY and us smiling; underneath the photograph was printed: *Jenny Harris, Mark Bolton and some of their helpers*, and a lot more besides, and it was a centre spread. "And I've brought you this. It's a small part of the insurance money for Jack," Samantha added and handed Jenny a cheque for £500. "I don't want another horse, not yet anyway, not when I'm still at boarding school. Daddy's hopeless at looking after anything and Mummy just isn't interested."

"But this is wonderful! Just wonderful! And just what we need," cried Jenny reading the cheque with moist eyes. "It's like a gift from heaven. Are you sure it's real?"she asked before leaning forward to kiss Samantha. "And of course you can help. We'll need every pair of hands available."

All day the telephone rang. Mrs Sykes rang to say that a home for horses would never work. Ron Redman

34

rang to ask whether we would be able to go on keeping his horses. A pensioner rang to say she was giving us her week's pension and a child rang and in a childish voice told us that she was sending us a month's pocket money.

Jenny ordered tons of hay and more feed. "It's a good beginning but it won't last," she said. And now even Mark looked happy.

Josh and I caught up Squid and Fidget and groomed them. They both have very short legs and large heads. Jenny says they were bred to work in the coal mines, even though ponies haven't worked in them for years. Their shoulders are short and strong and their necks thick. They are sturdy, strong and obstinate and will pass the largest tractor in the land without batting any eyelid. Squid is bay with an uneven splash of white on his face. Fidget is piebald. Looking at them Samantha said, "I do hope we're going to rescue some worthwhile animals. Anyone can see those two weren't meant to happen."

"All the more reason to love them. How would you like to be ugly and unwanted Samantha?" asked Josh.

"I wouldn't be, would I?" replied Samantha glibly. "I know I was wanted. My mother waited five years for me."

"Big deal. But the animals here are all treated the same," I said.

"So there," added Josh smiling.

From that moment I didn't like Samantha. I suppose I was jealous too for now she always seemed to be following Josh around. And she didn't really help, or only in fits and starts. Mostly she stood about, look-

35

ing critical, saying things like, "You've left some mud on Squid's hock," or "You've dropped some hay" - that sort of thing. But she never stooped to pick up anything. I don't think Samantha liked me much either. Sometimes she looked at me with the eyes of a snarling cat. She was always well turned out; her jeans had the right label on them, and her jerseys were the sort which cost £100 a piece. Sometimes I felt like Squid and Fidget for I too had a short neck and was small for my age.

Later that day Josh and I lunged Squid and Fidget in the covered school which had part of the roof missing, so let the rain in. Watching us Samantha said, "Why are you doing that for goodness sake?"

Josh explained that we were getting them ready for new homes. "They are on the rehousing list, because with only thirty acres we must keep making room for the newcomers," he added.

"But who on earth will want them?" replied Samantha laughing.

"Someone," said Josh.

The ponies lunged beautifully. I think they enjoyed the attention. We did the same with lop-eared, long-backed Fantasy; and grey Trooper who for some reason always made me think of a wrung out dishcloth, the stringy sort.

"I don't think I would want any of them actually," said Samantha as we stood in the middle of the covered school, patting Trooper. "None of them would win a prize for anything as far as I can see. Why don't you rescue more worthwhile animals - a few thoroughbreds for instance?" asked Samantha seriously.

"Perhaps they don't need rescuing. We've only just opened; have a heart," said Josh.

And then of course Samantha wanted to try lungeing; and though Trooper had done enough, Josh gave her a lesson just the same, explaining how you make a V shape with the whip in one hand, the rein in the other and the horse in the sharp piece and how you keep moving all the time.

And I thought, that's how it's going to be, Samantha's going to pick the nice jobs, never the dirty ones!

Outside Jenny was grooming Secret. "What's the matter? Why the glum face?" she asked. "Is everything all right Cathy?"

"Yes, except that Samantha's taking over," I answered.

"Give her time to settle in, Cathy; she'll change. Oh you're not jealous are you because you know we all love you?" said Jenny giving me a hug. And then appearing from nowhere Mark said, "No vendettas here please. Samantha's a smashing kid."

"Except for Jack," I replied. "You seem to have forgotten Jack already. Personally, I shall never forgive her for that, never ever."

"Oh hurray, here comes the hay," cried Jenny sounding glad to change the subject. "All thanks to Samantha."

"You mean Jack," I said. "You mean conscience money Jenny, don't you?"

When Samantha saw the hay, she pleaded that she had a bad back. "But I'll count the bales if you like," she offered. Next she asked to be called Sammy. "All my school friends do," she said.

Soon after the hay was stacked, Barney Banks appeared looking incredibly handsome. "I saw the bit about this place becoming a sanctuary, Jenny. Does this mean you can't keep my horses any more?" he asked.

Jenny told him that there wasn't a problem, but could he pay his account on time in future and though she knew that being a TV star was hectic, his horses had to eat.

And all the time Samantha, whom I will now call Sammy was staring at him. "It is him, isn't it? It is the famous Barney Banks? Oh wow!" she cried.

Josh nodded.

"Oh you just wait till I tell the kids at school about meeting him. They simply won't believe me. If only I had my camera," Sammy gushed. She took a piece of paper from her pocket and smiling broadly asked him for his autograph. "You see you've been my hero ever since I can remember. I never thought I would meet you, not in my wildest dreams. Not like this. It's fantastic," she cried.

"It's a pleasure," said Barney Banks. And for the first time I realised how handsome he really was, for until this moment he had seemed like everyone else. In fact I had found him rather feeble, because he was unable to adjust a bridle properly, and twice he had ridden out with a twisted girth.

"People will pay to come here and see your horses, I know they will," continued Sammy. "Oh wow, thanks a million. I have always watched your programme and so have my friends, it's really great," she continued taking back the piece of paper, folding it carefully, adding. "I really will treasure this - I won't sell it however much I'm bid." Sammy helped Barney Banks tack up his two grey horses. Then they rode away together chattering like old friends.

"She doesn't waste much time does she?" asked Josh.

"She'll go far," said Jenny smiling.

"And how," added Josh laughing.

At that moment I wished more than anything else that I had a dog. I wanted to bury my nose in a dog's fur and know that whatever I did or said, I would still be loved. Then I thought that even a dog might love Sammy more, particularly if her pockets were full of doggy chocs. And then I knew I hated her and that nothing would change it. I thought, Mum would call it a clash of personalities, but it's worse than that, and it's not just jealousy either; it's because I feel like a poor relation when she's around and it's what she says as well. I can't accept her views and then there's Jack's ghost which haunts me. "Just a horse," her father said. But he was beautiful and young and full of life before she had him. I was still thinking like this, brooding, Mum would have called it, when an elderly man appeared in a truck and leaning out called, "Is this the Horse Sanctuary?"

"Sure. Help yourself. Who do you want?" I asked.

"The owner. The manager. Oh, I don't know, just anyone. The name's Bill," he said leaning out to shake my hand. "I love horses and I want to help."

I shouted to Jenny, "We've got a new helper here."

They shook hands. He explained that he was a builder, but retired now. "Since my wife died, I need something to occupy my mind," he said. "And I grew up with horses. Will you have me? I'm pretty handy with a hammer."

"Have you? Of course we will," cried Jenny. "All are welcome."

"I'm not too old then?" There was mirth in Bill's grey eyes as he spoke.

"Too old! Nobody's too old to help here," said Jenny. "Look around. See what you think about the place."

"Come and see Fantasy and Trooper," I said.

But Bill was really more interested in the buildings than the horses. After a few minutes he said, "What about that big building over there? It looks a bit ropey to me."

"It's the covered school; it leaks," I said.

"That's what I thought. I'll just measure it up. I've got some tin at home which will be just the job my darling," he said. I liked Bill straightaway, though I wished he wouldn't call me 'my darling.' The horses seemed to like him too. I soon discovered that he was the kindest person I had ever met. His wife had died three years ago, so he was often lonely. Soon HORSEHAVEN meant a lot to him, almost as much as it meant to me.

Sarah and Gillian arrived and gave us all posters to stick up. They said BOOT SALE, DON'T MISS IT. IN AID OF SUFFERING AND ABANDONED HORSES. Just £5 a pitch. £6 on the day - with their address and telephone number on the bottom.

Barney Banks and Samantha returned, with Secret and Mystery dripping with sweat. "Wow, that was the best ride ever. It really was fantastic. You just wait till I tell my friends at school that I've been riding with Barney Banks. Their faces will turn green with envy," cried Sammy.

"We must do it again," said Barney Banks smiling at her.

"Again! Wow, how fantastic. I really will look forward to that," gushed Sammy.

As Josh and I rubbed down Mystery and Secret, before putting straw on their backs and their rugs the wrong way up, Josh said, "We could all learn something about public relations from Sammy. You particularly Cathy. Sometimes you're so remote and when you are like that, people think you're superior. Better to talk rubbish like Sammy than not at all. What do you think?"

"I don't think. I just work. Which is more than you can say of Sammy," I answered.

"But in spite of that she keeps winning."

Of course Josh was right. I wasn't outgoing enough. I was afraid of being rebuffed but I wasn't going to admit it, so I said instead in an icy voice, "Can't you understand? I don't want to be like her. Just remember what happened to Jack, will you?"

"That wasn't all her fault."

"Oh yeah," I answered.

We were getting near to quarrelling which had never happened before. Then Josh laughed. "If only you each had a bit of each other in you, you'd both be perfect," he said.

But it didn't seem like a laughing matter to me, so I went away and held nails for Bill who was already working on the covered school. Then still disheartened, I wandered down to the bottom field to look at the polo ponies. They were all right except for Queenie who was still lame. She was small for a polo pony and liver chestnut with a star. She had slender thorough-bred legs. I remembered then that Ron Redman had said that if she wasn't sound by Christmas she would have to go for meat, and I felt a cold shiver of fear for her run down my back. Among the polo ponies she was bottom of the pecking order; and though she had once been one of the best polo ponies in England, work had taken its toll, so that now her fetlocks were lumpy with windgalls and she had a couple of splints on her cannon bones. She had been Ron Redman's champion polo pony; he had scored more goals on her than on any other pony. Unfortunately Ron only saw ponies as things you used, throwaway objects, and more than once, I had heard him say, "I'm not sentimental about animals. I can't afford to be; they are my business, and if my ponies can't come up with the goods, it's either the sale ring, or curtains for them." He seemed to think the same about wives, for he had had three to date and was barely forty.

In the nearby village of Treadmill, bells were ring-ing for evensong. I put my arms around Queenie's muddy neck and said, "I won't let you go for meat, okay?" And she nuzzled my cheek and blew in my hair and the bells went on ringing across fields call-ing the good to prayer. I knew then that I couldn't be like Sammy even if I wanted to be. I just wasn't made that way. I was too shy for one thing and I wasn't as confident as she was; she expected everyone to like her.

CHAPTER FIVE

FANTASY GOES

At half past eight on Saturday morning, cars started to arrive for the boot sale. Josh, Jenny and I had been up since first light grooming, mucking out and generally sprucing up the place. Now my arms ached and my head buzzed with a mixture of excitement, trepidation and exhaustion, for this was to be our first fund raising event and because of that was of great significance, and for many it would be their first glimpse of HORSEHAVEN.

"We really should have some bad cases on show," said Jenny.

Mark stood at the gate collecting money both from car boot owners who had not paid already and from people who had come to buy. Soon Gillian and Sarah arrived with their mother, a small bustling person who rushed from car to car asking the owners whether they needed anything. By this time Bill was erecting a huge sign which read HORSEHAVON and no one had the heart to tell him that he had spelt HORSEHAVEN wrong.

Mrs Sykes arrived at nine o'clock demanding to be told what was going on. "If this continues, I'll have to remove Romance. I don't want to, but it's really too much," she fumed.

"Don't worry Mrs S, this is a one off," replied Josh carrying her saddle for her.

"You don't like it being a Horse Sanctuary then?" I asked.

"No I do not. I don't like crowds for a start and that man at the gate tried to take 50p off me, and the spelling on the noticeboard is all wrong and since when did this place become HORSEHAVEN. That's what I want to know."

"Just a few days back," said Josh bridling Romance. "Don't you like horses then Mrs S?"

"Of course I do, and there's no need to be saucy, Josh. I'm one of the few people here who pays their livery charges on time."

I held her stirrup while she mounted. "There we go," I said, which was what everyone seemed to be saying at that time.

"I shall have to ride in the school. I can't get through that crowd. Open the doors will you Josh?" demanded Mrs Sykes.

Soon people were asking why there wasn't any food on sale.

"Not even a cup of tea," moaned an immensely large woman clutching the hands of two small children.

"Not even a raffle. This is a funny sort of boot sale," said someone else.

"50p to come in and not a scrap to eat."

"It's disgusting."

The crowd surged around the horses handing them titbits.

Romance was back in his box by this time with Mrs Sykes standing outside. "Not this one, don't feed this one. He's not a rescued horse. He cost me £3,000," she said.

Josh and I couldn't help laughing as we watched her. "£3,000!" exclaimed Josh. "It's an awful lot for a horse like Romance."

"Not if he's what you want. And he is perfect for Mrs Sykes," I answered. "Most horses wouldn't put up with doing the same dressage again and again, they would mutiny."

At three o'clock, cars started to leave. By four o'clock there was just us left.

We went inside to count the money we had made. There was £80 from the cars, £50 from visitors and £90 in donations.

"We should have had teas," I said.

"And a hamburger stall," said Josh.

"And biscuits," I added.

"We'll do it better next time," Jenny told us. "Anyway the result is marvellous - £220. We'll definitely have it again."

"I know we should have had a raffle, but there wasn't time to organise it, and Mum thought that only a few people would turn up," apologised Gillian.

"But it's a wonderful result, just wonderful," cried Jenny hugging her. "Please don't apologise. It surpassed my wildest dreams."

But I could only think that we had made less than half the amount Sammy had given us, and it spoilt everything.

It was dark when I rode my bike home. When I reached Cowford there were boys standing at a street corner. They linked arms across the road and called, "How about a cuddle darling," and I felt fear trickle down my spine like ice.

"I'm in a hurry," I said. "I'm late already." I knew at least one of them; he was in his last year at school but was rarely there. I tried to control my fear as one does with a vicious, crazy or simply upset horse, for animals can smell fear.

"Where have you been then?" asked a tall boy with a brutal face.

"She's called Cathy," said the boy I knew. "And she's not interested in boys."

"I've been to the stables, I help there, now please let me through. My Mum will be sending the police out to look for me soon, she's that anxious. She is really, so's my Dad, real neurotic he is." I was slipping into the way they talked, the way one talked at school, if one wanted to be accepted there. But I was still afraid.

But now they burst out laughing. "She's been to the stables then," laughed the one I knew.

"And she smells like it," said another.

And then I was through, standing on my pedals longing to be home.

Mum was standing outside our house waiting for me. "Oh there you are. I've been so worried. Why are you so late?" she cried.

And because I was still afraid I promised not to stay out late again, while it was dark so early.

"Perhaps Mark will run me home another time," I

said hopefully, before hugging Mum because she looked tired. "You mustn't worry so. I'm not a fool Mum. I can cope," I added.

But Mum only quoted, "Famous last words," and said that it wasn't just fools who got mugged, but ordinary decent folk who had never hurt anyone. And then Dad appeared and went on and on about me being out in the dark until finally I reacted by saying, "It's not my fault we haven't got a car." And then Dad, having no answer, sent me to my room.

I thought Sunday would be peaceful but it wasn't. When I arrived at HORSEHAVEN I found Fantasy tied up in the yard. Josh was picking out his hoofs.

"He's going. There's some people coming to look at him. Jenny says it sounds a perfect home," said Josh without enthusiasm.

"They may not like his lop ears," I suggested hopefully.

"She's told them about his ears."

"And about his long back?"

"Sure. I heard her. She said that he was really ugly, but they still want him,' said Josh gloomily.

"Stop the gloom. We agreed we would rehome our horses. How else can we keep more," said Jenny appearing from the house.

"But it's so soon. I mean we've only just become a Sanctuary," I answered. "And shouldn't we inspect their place first?"

"Let me be the judge of that," replied Jenny.

I knew I would miss Fantasy. He wasn't a good ride, his back was too long for that, but he was always the same - kind, patient and polite and how many humans are that?

"Jenny says we can inspect whenever we like," said Josh as Jenny went to answer a telephone call. "All right Cathy?"

I didn't answer. I knew I would miss Fantasy's crazy lop ears and welcoming whinny. Josh wouldn't look at me. He was angry and upset and maybe he was crying too.

Fantasy's prospective owners arrived in a Land Rover - a tall man in a waxed jacket and green wellies, a woman also in wellies with a scarf over her head, and a small bubbly child. Straightaway they rushed up to Fantasy crying, "Is this the one?"

"Oh I do love his ears," cried the woman. "They look so original."

"And he's so friendly," said the child who was around seven years old and called Becky.

"Has he got a good temperament?" the man asked Josh.

"Middling to bad," lied Josh.

"Don't listen Maurice. Anyone can see that the lad doesn't want us to have him," laughed the woman. And then they all laughed, the little girl squealing like a piglet.

Jenny appeared and shaking them by the hand said, "You know you are only having Fantasy for a trial period. We are not selling him or giving him away, and we can fetch him back here at any time. We've drawn up an agreement for you to sign if you decide you want him."

"Why do you want him?" I asked Becky.

"So that Mum can ride with me. You see I've got a

pony called Shambles and he needs a friend. Mum won't be riding very often, because she works part time. But it will be lovely to go for long rides sometimes and take a picnic."

I must say the more we listened the more perfect the home sounded. The people were called Mackintosh and they seemed to have plenty of money plus a paddock and three loose-boxes. Jenny asked lots of tricky questions; how often does a horse need worming was one and what causes laminitis another. Mrs Mackintosh knew all the answers , while Becky wandered around admiring everything. Then Mrs Mackintosh rode Fantasy briefly in the covered school, which, thanks to Bill, had stopped leaking and she said that Fantasy was exactly what she wanted. After that they went indoors with Jenny to have a coffee and sign the contract.

"You're not crying are you Cathy?" asked Josh accusingly.

"No, I thought you were. I'll miss him," I said.

"Same here. The lesson is don't get too fond of anything," said Josh bitterly.

"Not ever?" I laughed.

Josh nodded.

"But he'll have a lovely home," I said.

"Sure," said Josh. "Let's hope it stays that way."

We bandaged Fantasy's legs and loaded him. Trooper neighed frantically from his loose-box. Squid and Fidget neighed from the paddock by the house. Fantasy looked round anxiously and I could see that he didn't want to leave.

"You're going to have a lovely home," I told him pat-

49

ting his trembling neck.

"We don't know how to thank you," said Mrs Mackintosh to Jenny as she climbed into the Land Rover.

"Well don't then. I do hope you get on with him. If you don't, we're as near as a phone call," said Jenny blowing her nose. "Don't forget now. If anything happens and you can't cope, he's to come straight back, no hassle, we'll always have room for him; and technically he's still ours."

"Message received and understood," replied Mr Mackintosh briskly, starting the Land Rover.

We watched them drive away. The sun was shining, but I felt cold just the same.

"I hope we've done the right thing," said Josh.

"Of course we have," replied Jenny.

"We can't afford to be sentimental. We must be realistic, it's what we're here for - to find poor horses a new life. Don't spoil it." Mark spoke glibly, but he wasn't horsey so he could hardly be expected to understand how miserable we felt at that moment.

"I just wish we had looked at the home first," said Josh slowly.

Trooper was restless all day. Bill appeared and started mending fences. What was Fantasy thinking now? Was he all right? I wondered, handing Bill a mallet. Later we removed Fantasy's name from his loose-box door.

"I hope we can see him soon," I said.

"Not for a week or two. We must give him time to settle in," replied Jenny. "And it's quite a way."

But life took over. We kept meaning to go, but there was never time. I've been told that 'the road to hell is paved with good intentions', and that's how it felt afterwards, when we were all eaten up with remorse; but that comes later.

A lot of things happened before we went to see Fantasy, some good, some bad, and all the time we seemed to be perched on the edge of bankruptcy and that was perhaps the worst thing of all. For we would have gone to see Fantasy earlier if Jenny had had the money for petrol, and then Mark's car failed its MOT, and that caused a lot more hassle and expense. Then Ron Redman wrote to say that we were to have Queenie put down and use the money she fetched to pay his bill. I howled all night after Jenny got the letter. It had an Argentinean stamp on it, because Ron was there buying new polo ponies for the approaching season, and we couldn't reach him even if we wanted to, not until April. Meanwhile his ponies, who weren't ponies in the true sense being over fifteen hands high, were eating all the hay in the barn. And we all knew that Jenny would never bring herself to take Queenie to the abattoir.

I was staying so long helping at weekends now that on Saturdays Jenny let me sleep in a room at the back of her house. It wasn't much of a room, but it was better than biking through Cowford in the dark with people coming out of pubs in droves, and it kept Mum and Dad happy. If Josh was very late his mother would pick him up in her car, sometimes coming straight from the hospital still in her nurse's uniform. Gillian and Sarah always had to be home for tea. They lived a well regulated life and, though they were fond of the horses, they were not fanatics like me and Josh.

Home came first with them, whereas with me it was a poor second. Josh's house was often empty because his mother worked such long hours and his Dad was still away, so it didn't rate very highly either. In fact he often said that like me, he wouldn't have been able to survive without Horsehaven.

The room at the back of Jenny's house had once been the grooms' mess room, that was when people could afford grooms, and long before Jenny acquired the house. It was empty now except for a sagging chair, a table and an electric light in the centre dangling from the ceiling without a shade. And there was dust and cobwebs everywhere. Josh and I swept it out. From somewhere Jenny produced a put-up bed. I brought my collection of china horses from home and put them on the window sill, and Josh gave me a poster with galloping horses on it to cover a bare piece of wall. But really the state of the room didn't bother me, because when I got into bed at night I always fell asleep straightaway; and when I wakened on Sunday mornings it was to leap straight up and rush outside to feed the horses. So I was immensely happy to have the room; and it made my life much easier.

CHAPTER SIX

FOUR LITTLE PONIES

School was even worse than usual; boys taunted me because I didn't want to go with them. A lesson on weather was ruined by a boy called Kevin going crazy and smashing a thermometer. Someone wolfed down my lunch when I wasn't looking, and one of the teachers told me that my hair was like a pony's mane and when was I going to do something about it?

I said that since I loved ponies, I didn't mind and then she said she would be writing to my mother. And it rained and rained, lashing the huge plate glass form room windows and rattling the roof of the bike shed. Finally a boy called Nathan was suspended and a girl called Jane taken home because she had a raging temperature. After that things grew a little calmer. But one way and another I was overjoyed when Saturday came round again for compared to school Horsehaven seemed like heaven. It was November now and when the day's work was done we sat in the tack room talking, Jenny said that donations were still dribbling in. But Mark replied that it just wasn't enough and that we must do something spectacular soon, something which would really put us on the map.

"When my father returns he will be full of ideas," said Josh hopefully. He had said this before many times; until now I had wondered whether his father would ever return. The rain stopped falling and the first frosts of winter made icicles on the window ledge of my room. Because of this I slept in a clean track suit and filled up a hot water bottle and took it to bed with me on Saturday nights.

Later on this particular day, Jenny came running into the tack room calling, "An old lady has just rung, she sounds frantic. She wants us to fetch her ponies at once. She says they're starving. I've got the address here." She waved a bit of paper under Mark's nose and added, "Action stations. Come on, get moving." And now we ran in all directions. Josh bedded down the trailer. Mark started the car. I fetched headcollars and two buckets of feed. Gillian and Sarah filled two haynets with hay, asking at the same time, "We won't be very late will we?"

"I shouldn't think so. It's not that far," replied Jenny, fetching gloves and a road atlas from the house. I sat in the back with Sarah on my knee and it felt lovely to be actually doing something really worthwhile at last.

"I hope there are only two ponies. I don't want to make the journey more than once; this car wasn't designed to pull a trailer," Mark said. And now freezing drizzle fell from a gloomy sky. "We need a horse box," he continued. "One for five horses, a new one." He was right of course, but we needed so many things

- more feed bins, more straw, bales of shavings; the list was endless.

"We'll hold a jumble sale; jumble sales make lots of money," suggested Gillian. "Enough to buy a new horse box," cried Sarah hoping to please Mark, whom she adored.

"We'll have a cake stall," said Gillian.

"And a raffle," added Josh.

"And cups of tea and biscuits and a hamburger stall," I said beginning to laugh.

"Everything will be easier when we're a registered charity," Jenny said.

"Then we'll dress Fidget and Squid up and take them into Cowford with collecting boxes on Christmas Eve," Mark suggested.

The rain on the windows made the car seem smaller than it was. I felt claustrophobic. I wished now that I had stayed behind. Soon Mark's car was struggling up hills, groaning like an animal in pain and I couldn't help wondering how it would make the journey back with ponies on board.

At last we turned down a lane.

"It's really isolated isn't it?" asked Josh.

"That's how she said it would be, at the back of no-where, she called it," replied Jenny, before we saw an old lady standing by a gate wearing a felt hat, and a mackintosh held together by binder twine, flagging us down. We stopped. She tapped on the driver's window and called, "Follow me down the lane." She hadn't any teeth and I remember thinking, I hope I never look like her. I hope I die before I get too old.

We stopped at the end of the lane. The ground

squelched beneath our feet. It was still raining.

"How am I going to turn?" wailed Mark.

"Before we load up. I'll help you," said Jenny.

We all helped. We turned the car, first unhitching the trailer and then we turned that too before rehitching it to the car. When it was done, we were all sweating.

"The name is Flora Duckett," said the old woman holding out a cracked hand wearing a mitten, the fingerless sort. I didn't shake it for I was already hurrying towards the field looking through the murk for the ponies.

"I'm so ashamed. I thought my daughter and son-in-law were looking after my ponies. Finding them like this has been a great shock," said Flora Duckett.

Mist blew like smoke across the field. Each footstep left a pool of water in its wake. Mark had stayed by the car and I couldn't blame him, for only a horsey person would have gone on in the rain and mist and gathering darkness; only a horsey person or a mad one.

"When I came down here yesterday and saw them I felt so ill; I thought I was going to have a heart attack, it was as bad as that," said the old lady. "I've had two heart attacks already."

But I wasn't listening to Flora Duckett now, for I hated everything about her. All I wanted to see was the ponies. I know it wasn't nice of me but that's the way it was. In fact as I stood in that field staring into the distance I was thinking, 'Stupid old hag!' And hating myself for thinking it. Then we saw them coming towards us - four little ponies, as thin as toast racks walking on pathetic misshapen hoofs.

"You see I haven't been down here for six months, not till yesterday. I'm feeling a bit shaky, may I sit in your car?" asked Flora Duckett.

Mark helped her to his car. Once inside she called in a crackly voice, "I saved them from slaughter. They were being loaded onto a meat lorry."

Silently I fetched the buckets of feed from the trailer. The ponies fought to get their noses inside them. There was no flesh between their ribs; their coats were mangy and even in the rain, I could see hungry, blood sucking lice clustered around their ears. Their hoofs were so long that they really were walking on their heels.

We put headcollars on three of the ponies, while Jenny called in an angry voice, "Where are your children Mrs Duckett? I would like a word with them."

"I don't know. They went away without telling me, the scum. They just turned their dogs loose and went. I would like to crucify them," she called back.

"They went, just like that?" muttered Mark.

"Which are we taking, because we can't take them all," asked Josh.

"Just two this journey. We'll leave the haynets for the two we don't take," decided Jenny. "We'll come back for them later."

"Straightaway! It must be straightaway," I said, "because they can't stay here a minute longer."

"Bless you for coming. I saw the bit about you in my paper and I knew you wouldn't let me down. I think you are wonderful, wonderful people. The salt of the earth," called Flora Duckett from the car.

None of us felt like talking. Some things are too bad for words and this was one of them. In silence, we chose the two smallest ponies. Their heads were too tiny for the headcollars we had brought; fortunately they were made of nylon and we could tie knots in them. One had a small star on his forehead and there was a little mare with a pale mane, and a tiny bay. But it was difficult to see more because they were covered with mud and matted hair, and their tails were almost on the ground, while their manes covered their entire necks. I had kept back some feed and they were so hungry that they rushed after it into the trailer while the two we were leaving behind neighed pathetically from the field. Our hands were freezing now and still none of us spoke. Silently Jenny hung the two haynets on the gate, while Josh and I threw up the ramp on the trailer and fastened it. Flora Duckett stayed in the car while Mark drove it up the lane. She got out at some crossroads and, as we clambered back into the car, she shouted again, "You're wonderful wonderful people."

"I never knew a pony could look as bad as these," I said after a time trying not to hear the engine struggling in Mark's car.

"No one could see them, their field was so isolated. I expect people only go that way in the summer and there was a notice saying, TRESPASSERS WILL BE PROSECUTED, though I don't suppose you saw it," said Jenny.

"I was too busy looking for the ponies to see anything else and then too upset," I said.

"Someone should be prosecuted," announced Gillian.

"They don't look like real ponies, they look like ponies made out of rags," sobbed Sarah.

"It's disgusting, absolutely disgusting," continued Gillian sounding like her mother. "Such things shouldn't be allowed to happen in a civilised country. Why didn't the RSPCA do something? I'm always sending them things."

"Their inspectors can't be everywhere at once, and if no one told them they were in the field, how were they to know?" I asked.

"It's still disgusting," said Gillian.

"They've got lice, they're riddled with worms; they'll have to be isolated," said Jenny thinking aloud.

"And we've still got to go back for the other two," Josh reminded us.

"If this car makes it home," said Mark.

After two miles the windscreen wipers packed up. Another ten and the clutch was slipping. It wasn't the car's fault. It had not been made to pull a trailer and it was old, very old. Presently it gave a sickening jolt and stopped altogether. Mark got out and kicked the front bumper. Smoke rose from the bonnet. Mark threw it open, while inside the trailer the ponies gave small half-hearted whinnies.

"Stupid old woman," shouted Josh getting out. "Why didn't she send them to us by horse box? I bet she's got masses of money stashed away in cardboard boxes."

"Under her bed," cried Sarah.

"Shut up. You're being horrible," cried Gillian. "One day you'll be old and decrepit. Can't we call the AA, Mark?" she went on. "They'll get us going again."

Mark shook his head. I knew that he had never had enough money to join anything. But Gillian's parents are the sort of people who are members of all the right things; sensible and well-organised, they buy a new car every other year and wouldn't be seen dead in Mark's old banger. Just occasionally I wish my parents were the same.

Eventually the car started again. I don't know what Mark did to it. The rain stopped and everything began to seem better.

"The old girl said that all their names began with T, but I've forgotten what they were," said Mark driving on.

"Topsy, Tim, Tommy and Tiddles," said Josh.

"We can give them new names," said Gillian, "because obviously they don't know their names poor things."

"When we return to fetch the others, we'll ask Mrs Duckett to sign a statement or she might want them back next week; or when they are really well again. and that would be a disaster," said Jenny.

"They are not going to die? They are going to live, aren't they?" I asked next.

"Yes, but whether they ever become worth anything remains to be seen. They look stunted to me and their hoofs are going to take years to recover," replied Jenny sadly.

"I think Flora Duckett should be in a home where she's looked after twenty-four hours a day and bathed regularly," Gillian said.

"I don't suppose she wants to go into a home. She probably lives in a tumbledown cottage with twenty cats," said Jenny.

"And ten dogs," added Josh.

And now suddenly we were laughing, though with hindsight what we said next wasn't funny at all.

"And with stick insects and a poor budgie in a cage," cried Sarah.

"And mice everywhere," I added.

"And spiders in corners," said Josh. "Great big ones, the sort which make you scream Cathy."

"And fleas everywhere," added Sarah.

"Now you're being horrid again, and if you go on I'll never speak to any of you again," said Gillian in a headmistressy sort of voice. But now we couldn't stop. We had been wound up by misery for so long that we were now like a dammed up river which has burst its banks.

"And a sink piled high with dirty plates," Josh went on.

"And stained old chipped mugs," cried Sarah.

"And all the drains blocked," I added.

"And the toilet," cried Sarah. "It's really smelly."

"Stop it Sarah. No one can help being old. We'll all be old one day," said Gillian.

"And all the soot's come down the chimney. And no one's swept it up," cried Sarah unabashed going into peals of laughter.

"And the bath's overflowed and the water's running down the stairs," I said. "And there's rotting food everywhere.

"And dead mice," added Sarah.

But now at last we were home. We were greeted by neighing and the rattling of doors; because it was past feed time. And the polo ponies were milling around the gate fighting for the best view of the stables.

CHAPTER SEVEN

"WE'LL FIND THEM ..."

When we let down the ramp, we found that the mare with the pale mane had collapsed on the straw. Mark and Jenny half carried her out into the yard, while Sarah said, "Is she dead?" We stopped laughing abruptly.

"No, she's just exhausted," Josh said.

We put the ponies in the foaling box and bedded it down with straw which they immediately started to eat. We gave them buckets of water and half a bale of our best hay.

When they were settled and all eating, Jenny said, "Mark and I will go for the others now. First listen to what I have to say - please. We are going to save these poor ponies; they are all young. I haven't looked at their teeth yet, but I reckon they are probably all around four years old. They do have a great many things wrong with them. They are too weak to fight with one another, so we will leave them together for the time being, and there won't be any foals because the males have been gelded. (Sarah gave a disappointed groan at this moment). But because they have so many things wrong with them they must have their own set of grooming tools, and I've put these in their manger. And do wash your hands after you've been handling them; it's just a precaution really. Okay?" We all nodded and she went on. "Now I want them left alone to rest, and I want you all to go home as soon as possible. Tomorrow we'll groom and delouse them."

Gillian put up her hand as though at school. "But what about their feet Jenny? They can't walk properly. Every step must be agony," she said.

"And their fleas, what about them?" cried Sarah.

"They aren't fleas. Ponies don't have them. They're lice and I've just said that tomorrow we'll delouse them, and on Monday we'll have the farrier if he can come," said Jenny.

All this time Mark had been tinkering with his car. "Are we ready to go Jenny?" he asked, "because it's getting dark, or haven't you noticed?"

I pleaded to go with them, but Mark said he had to keep the car as light as possible if they weren't to break down again. Jenny put a thermos of coffee and some chocolate on the back seat.

"At least we know the way this time," Mark said.

"But we must find Flora Duckett and get her to sign away the ponies; otherwise we could be in trouble, especially if her awful daughter and son-in-law return home and need money," insisted Jenny.

"Take care," I said.

"We won't be late. Look after things, and go home before dark, those of you who are going home," called

Jenny as they left.

Saying that we might need evidence for a court case, Josh went home for his camera. I took some hay to the polo ponies. They were soaking wet and covered in mud, but their ears were warm and none of them was shivering.

Josh returned and we took photographs of the ponies in the loose-box. They had stopped eating. They weren't very big. I could see now that the mare with the pale mane was a palomino and that the other was bay. And then I looked at Fantasy's empty box and asked, "When can we see him? I miss him so much and sometimes Trooper looks so sad, I'm sure he's missing him too."

"I don't know - soon I hope," Josh said.

"We'll need someone to drive us. Mark's car's useless. What about your Mum?" I asked next. But Josh said that his mother was overworked and that they had not heard from his father for two weeks now, and that she couldn't take on any more, not while his father was still away. I wished then that I was grown up with my own car. We had eaten our sandwiches hours ago and after a time Josh went home. I went into Jenny's house and put tea ready on the table and still they hadn't returned.

I started to imagine all the things which might have gone wrong. I imagined a crash with the trailer turning over. I imagined the car's brakes snapping and it going down a hill at a hundred miles an hour and then crashing into a wall. I imagined Jenny dying and no more horses at HORSEHAVEN. Then I went outside and looked at the new arrivals. It was dark now and when I switched on the lights, they blinked and looked small and cuddly in spite of their bones jutting out.

Then I found Jenny's torch and took some hay to Squid and Fidget whom we had forgotten and they didn't shout at me because I was late, but gave little whinnies of thanks, and now it was quite dark and there was a fog coming down. I remembered Romance and gave him his special feed which was full of extra vitamins, though his coat gleamed like satin and he was overweight, so obviously didn't need them. I fed Trooper who was stabled now, and Secret and Mystery, who nearly pushed me over because I was late. And still Jenny and Mark had not returned. After that I tidied the tack room, and then I changed Romance's rugs which I had forgotten to do; and as I did up his surcingle, he bit my arm. Ignoring the pain, I put the stable tools away, because it was raining, and topped up water buckets. The little ponies were lying down, their poor misshapen hoofs tucked beneath them. I'd never seen ponies look so happy before. Their coats had dried and I could see that the bay really did have a dear little star on his forehead.

When I went indoors again the telephone was ringing, but it was only Mrs Sykes wanting to know whether Romance was all right. After that I sat in Jenny's small disordered kitchen and thought about money. I knew that however much we raised it would never be enough to save all the horses which needed saving. We needed a benefactor; but there wasn't one. Before I had thought any further the telephone rang again and this time it was Bill asking if everything was all right. I told him what had happened and he said not to worry, he would come right over in his trusty truck and then we would look for Jenny and Mark.

"Mark's car was never meant to pull a trailer," he said.

"You're telling me," I answered.

"Don't worry my darling; everything's going to be all right," said Bill soothingly before ringing off.

I sat and waited. I knew everything would be all right if Bill was coming. I knew he would find Mark and Jenny. He was simply that sort of person.

The funny thing was that as soon as I said, "The old lady who owned the ponies was called Flora Duckett," Bill knew who she was and where she lived.

We stood looking at the ponies and he said, "I've done work for her in the past, poor old lady. She must be old by now, really old."

I climbed into the truck. It was ancient, but cared for and loved, unlike Mark's car which lived in the rain and the wind, was rarely serviced and was certainly never loved.

"Don't look so sad, we'll find them my darling," Bill said.

"They left hours ago," I answered. "They should have been back long ago."

Bill knew the way. He was the sort of man who would always know the way. He drove the old truck lovingly, as a good rider nurses an old horse. He let her take her time up the hills, and when he changed gear it was gently done.

"Flora Duckett was a fine lady in her day, and a great

one for saving animals," he told me.

The rain spattered the windows. I thought, I'm glad Mum and Dad don't know I'm here in the wind and the rain with Bill looking for Mark and Jenny. I told Bill about the ponies and he said that he remembered Flora Duckett's children, a 'couple of layabouts' he called them, not worth a ten pence piece. Then he said that he was glad to be out doing something useful because he was sick of sitting by the fire watching the telly. "I rang you because I wanted to do something. And this is just the ticket," he said.

He had two children of his own, he told me, but his son was in the army and abroad and his daughter had married a man he didn't care for; and all the time while we talked, we were staring into the darkness and the rain hoping to see Mark's car and the trailer coming towards us.

Soon the roads were narrow and the signposts almost unreadable in the rain which even as we drove turned to sleet and then to hailstones as large as gobstoppers.

"Cheer up, we'll find them," Bill told me driving slower and slower while the hailstones fell on the truck like bullets from the sky.

And then at last we saw them; Mark's car was swivelled round half in a ditch, the trailer was lying sideways, and two small ponies were standing shivering on the verge, looking as though they had just swum across a river.

Bill said nothing. Silently we waved and got out. There was a police car parked nearby, and two police officers in yellow plastic jerkins, and Jenny with her fair hair hanging wet to her shoulders, and Mark holding his head in his hands.

"I've got a hitch, I've come to take the trailer home," said Bill in a matter of fact voice taking in the scene, digesting it. And then without another word he fetched a hammer from the truck, and started to mend the broken planks on the sides of the trailer. Jenny was shivering. She had one arm in a sling made out of a scarf. Mark looked angry. It was obvious he couldn't handle the police even though they were being helpful and offering to take Jenny home in the police car. Soon we were loading the ponies again. The little roan could hardly stagger by this time and coughed constantly. The police offered to call up our vet on their car radio. It was nine o'clock at night now and we were all freezing cold. Through chattering teeth Jenny thanked everyone, before climbing into the patrol car. " We're going home. Leave your car. Get in Mark," Bill said. "And Cathy, there's room for you both in the cab."

I think I slept on the way home, for it seemed but a moment between setting off and stepping out into the stable yard. Jenny was waiting for us. A vet was with her. They had made a loose-box ready for the two ponies. A moment later my parents appeared in a neighbour's car. "Are you all right Cath? We've been so worried. We telephoned and telephoned and there was never any answer," my mother called. And now I hated them for mixing up my two lives, three really if you count school - which I liked to keep in separate compartments.

"Of course I am. why do you fuss? You know I'm always here," I said.

Our elderly neighbours, Mr and Mrs Anders sighed and I guessed they were thinking, what a very disagreeable child, but aren't they all the same nowadays? No manners, not like we were, as different as chalk from cheese. And they have it so easy, too easy. They're spoilt, that's what it is, spoilt. But I knew it wasn't true. Sammy might be spoilt, but I wasn't, no way.

"You can go home. I'm staying. I'll see you tomorrow," I said.

Then Bill spoke. "Oh Cathy, where are your manners my darling?" he said. "Flown out of the window have they?" And now even he seemed against me.

The vet was examining the ponies, filling the little roan with antibiotics, saying that she had pneumonia and had had it for a long time and that two of the others had pleurisy. He said that they had been very neglected and someone should go to prison for it. Suddenly he was shaking with anger. And we were all so tired. I'd never been so tired before. Jenny was literally trembling with exhaustion and Bill was showing his age, while Mum said, "Oh well if you don't want us Cath, we may as well go home again," in an offended voice.

Then suddenly without realising it, I had my arms around Mum's neck and was hugging her. "I'm sorry. I don't mean to be like this, but it's been such a terrible day and I think two of the ponies will be dead by morning and it seems such a shame," I said.

At the same moment Josh appeared on his bike calling, "Are you all right? I rang a dozen times and couldn't get an answer."

"Oh no not you too!" cried Jenny.

Some time later everyone went home but me, Jenny and Mark. After that I stayed up with the little roan pony, listening to her breathing (which sounded like a rasp working on a door) and watching her sides going in and out like a bellows. For half an hour she lay with her head in my lap, and I thought she was about to die. I don't usually pray, but I prayed that night. Twice Jenny appeared to say, "Go to bed. I'll take over." But by this time I was too tired to move. At about two o'clock in the morning the pony stood up and almost immediately I fell into a relieved sleep in the corner of the loose-box, and woke much later to find Jenny feeding the pony out of a bucket. "I think she's going to live Cathy. I really do, and most of it's due to you," she said.

I was stiff with cold and my joints creaked as I stood up. My head ached. "What about the others?" I asked through chattering teeth.

"Them too. Come and look," said Jenny. The other three ponies were all together in the foaling box. They looked at me and wrinkled their dear little noses in welcome, and now their eyes were shining with contentment.

"The sight of them makes everything seem worthwhile doesn't it," asked Jenny.

I was crying again, but this time they were not tears of sorrow, but tears of joy. I wanted to shout to the world, the ponies are going to live; we've saved them. Jenny steered me into the house, handed me a hot water bottle and said, "Go to bed, you've done your share. The worst is over now."

"Except that we haven't a car any more," I said and tried to laugh.

"We'll get by, not to worry. We're still alive, that's what matters," said Jenny. "And we've saved four little ponies. Isn't that just wonderful? Isn't that what we're here for?"

I ate a bowlful of cereal and fell into bed. I must have fallen asleep immediately because the next thing I knew was Jenny appearing with breakfast on a tray.

"The ponies are fine," she told me, putting the tray on a table beside my bed. "Bill and Josh have deloused them, and the little roan is eating well." I was surprised to see breakfast on a tray - it had not happened to me since I had had measles at eight years old. Jenny drew back the curtains. Outside a faint sun shone uncertainly in a leaden sky.

"I've got great news for you," Jenny said smiling at me. "A treat. We're going to see Fantasy; Bill's taking us."

"Today? Really?"

"Yes, we're leaving quite soon and taking lunch. All the work's done outside. We thought you deserved a lie in." Jenny's arm was still in a sling. She was in tidy clothes.

"Are you all right? And what about Mark's car?" I asked sitting up.

"He's just leaving to take it to a dump. It skidded. It's a write-off. But don't let's talk about last night," she said going out, shutting the door after her.

Going to see Fantasy was as good as a sudden, unexpected present. I dressed quickly wishing that I had clean clothes to put on, for mine felt like the day before. I could hear Jenny humming as she prepared a picnic lunch in the kitchen. I thought of Fantasy, dear, funny, lop-eared, affectionate Fantasy, while outside the sky cleared and the sun took over the sky.

CHAPTER EIGHT

A DEPRESSING JOURNEY

"Do you think Fantasy will recognise us?" I asked.

"Of course," replied Josh with the utmost certainty.

We were rattling along in the back of Bill's truck. And though he drove at a steady forty five miles an hour, it was still a rough ride in the back. Gillian passed round a bag of sweets. We were all keyed up, for our lives suddenly seemed to be moving into the fast lane.

Barney Banks had agreed to make a speech on our first Open Day which was scheduled for just before Christmas. Squid and Fidget were to go round Cowford with collecting boxes, and next week Gillian and Sarah's Mum had organised a jumble sale in aid of Horsehaven. Gillian told us now that Treadmill Village Hall had been booked and that we were all expected to bring things and to help. I felt guilty because I had not put up any of the posters she had given me advertising the jumble sale. Josh said that he had got his Mum to put his up in the hospital where people waited to see specialists. "They are what's called a captive audience," he said happily. "So they should be successful."

Soon after that we stopped to eat the sandwiches Jenny had made. The sun was still shining, pale and sickly in the winter sky. "Only ten more miles," Jenny said.

I imagined Fantasy welcoming us, his lop ears forward, his eyes shining, his nose nickering a welcome. He had been my favourite horse at the stables for a long time. "You'll love Fantasy," I told Bill, eating a cheese and pickle sandwich. "He's such a character." Ten minutes later we climbed back into the truck. The heat from the heater did not reach to the back and we were all cold now. Josh said that the journey home would be even colder. I said that we would be warmed by our meeting with Fantasy.

Gillian and Sarah huddled together, their small faces pinched with cold. Traffic increased, a plane thundered overhead.

"Nearly there," called Jenny from the front.

We had all brought titbits for Fantasy.

"Drive faster Bill," I yelled, "or there will be four frozen corpses by the time you get there. Fantasy's probably clipped and wearing a posh rug," I continued, while Bill put his foot hard on the accelerator and the truck shook.

"It's so cold. I wish we hadn't come," announced Gillian miserably.

"We can go for a run when we get out," suggested Josh.

But now the truck had stopped. "I'm just looking at a map," called Jenny from the cab. "We're almost there."

"Famous last words," commented Gillian miserably.

"It's two o'clock. Did Jenny ring them?" asked Josh. "Because it'll be awful if they are out when we get there."

"But we can still see Fantasy," I answered.

"Not if she's out riding," Josh said.

The truck started again and then, quite soon stopped again. "I think we've arrived," called Jenny leaping out. "Now which is Prospect House?"

"That one," said Bill pointing. "Look there's a notice saying so."

"And another one," I added suddenly feeling very cold. "And it says, FOR SALE, and it's deserted," and now I felt completely empty inside.

"We must have come to the wrong place," replied Jenny in a bewildered voice.

"Let's look round the back for the loose-boxes they said they had," suggested Josh.

"The notice could be for the house next door," suggested Gillian hopefully.

Prospect House was completely empty, the doors locked. We found the loose-boxes at the back with padlocked doors. Everything was swept clean and so empty that one knew without asking that the owners were never coming back.

"How could they do it to us? How could they?" cried Jenny. "I told them we were as near as a telephone, and they signed the agreement."

"I knew we should have visited and taken up references," said Josh gloomily.

"I wanted to see Fantasy so much," wailed Sarah.

"He may be all right; they may have moved; they may be trying to telephone us at this very moment. We must not despair," said Jenny in a beleaguered sort of voice.

Banging his cold hands against his sides, Bill suggested that we made inquiries next door.

All the houses were new in the row which confronted us. Prospect House was by far the largest and the only one with any land. It looked glaringly red and lost in the grey November countryside. At this moment Gillian and Sarah returned to the truck like puppies with their tails between their legs. The rest of us waited while Jenny knocked on the door of a house called South Cote. After much rattling of chains and locks an elderly man opened it.

"We are looking for the Mackintoshes; they lived next door," said Jenny smiling.

"They had a black horse called Fantasy," I added quickly.

"And a pony called Shambles," said Josh.

"We remember them very well," said the man who had a bristling white moustache.

"Always quarrelling they were," added the woman who now appeared, adding, "Come in anyway. Don't stand out in the cold." We went inside and sat in tasselled armchairs. I wanted to blow my nose but didn't dare take a tissue from my pocket for fear that the porridge oats there meant for Fantasy, might spill on to the lush pink carpet.

"And they had a little girl," added Jenny as an afterthought.

"Called Becky."

"They've left, gone, flitted," said the man, "owing money to everyone including us. The house has been repossessed. They let us all down."

"And the black horse?" I cried. "The one with the funny ears?"

"Sold along with the pony to pay their creditors. He threw her out. I don't know where she and the little girl went," said the woman. "She took up with a lad young enough to be her son."

"So you don't know where she went?" asked Jenny sounding desperate.

"I've no idea. And I don't want to know," replied the woman in a disapproving voice.

We thanked them and went outside again. The day seemed greyer than ever now and there did not seem a splinter of hope anywhere.

Looking at our defeated faces Bill said, "No luck then?"

Jenny shook her head. We piled back into the hateful truck. Josh told Gillian and Sarah what we had learnt. But I think they were too cold to take it in, for they said nothing.

"It's our fault. We should have checked them out," said Josh in an anguished voice. "We should have telephoned before we came. We've been idiots."

We knew it was Jenny's fault, because she was grown up and in control. She had let us down and even worse she had let down Fantasy. But we didn't blame her, because we all make mistakes.

"We may still find him," I said without much hope.

"Yeah, in a tin of dog meat," answered Josh.

"Or as a steak in a butcher's shop in France," I suggested.

"Stop it," cried Gillian putting her hands over her ears. "Just stop it."

It was a terrible journey home. Bill stopped the truck outside a roadside cafe and treated us all to hot drinks. Everyone there seemed to be looking at us, and Sarah wouldn't stop crying which hardly helped. Then Josh had a go at Jenny saying that everything was her fault, and Bill told Josh to mind his manners, and to remember that he was speaking to a lady. Worst of all, when we reached home, there was still the work to be done; horses brought in, rugs changed, muck picked up, horses fed and watered, the yard swept. Gillian and Sarah went home as soon as we arrived back.

The little ponies welcomed us. The roan mare was steady on her poor misshapen hoofs now and her breathing was nearly normal, but most of the time she stood in the far corner of her loose-box with her haunches hunched as though against a wind. Jenny took her temperature and said that it was still too high. Finally, at six o'clock I set off for home, still feeling hollow inside, still unable to look at Fantasy's loose-box without a sharp stab of pain, while my mind kept saying to me, if only - if only we had asked more questions, if only we had talked to the neighbours first, had been less trusting. I had had reservations about Mr Mackintosh and had said nothing. Why? I asked myself now. Then I thought, never again Cathy. Speak out next time. Say whatever you think always. 'Be counted' as Mum would say. But it didn't help. With Fantasy gone probably for ever, the town looked drabber, the boys hanging around a bus shelter more threatening, the air more polluted. Oh Fantasy my heart cried out, "Why did we let you go?"

When she saw me, Mum asked, "Are you all right? You look frozen to death."

"I am frozen, inside and out," I replied. "We've lost Fantasy. He's been sold, and I don't think we'll ever find him. I think he's in a tin of dog meat by now."

"Well, that's better than suffering somewhere out in the wind and the cold with nothing to eat Cathy, isn't it?" asked Mum handing me a mugful of coffee. "There, get this inside you and you'll feel better. You look half dead to me." And then I thought, if other horses are going to disappear like Fantasy, I don't think I want to go on, and that was the worst thought of all.

CHAPTER NINE

OUR LUCK CHANGES

Now we all began searching for the Mackintoshes. One evening Josh and I sat in his living room, which had patio windows into the garden and deep armchairs and reading lamps placed on low tables. One by one we rang every Mackintosh in the telephone directory. Each time we asked to speak to a Mrs Mackintosh who had a little girl called Becky. Most people were helpful though there were two rude replies. But worst of all there was not a single clue.

"Perhaps she wasn't Mrs Mackintosh after all?" suggested Josh.

"Or was ex directory," I replied.

We drank coffee and I said, "What about the expense, won't your Mum be furious when the telephone bill arrives?"

Josh said that she would create, but then she was always creating about something or other, but mostly about his Dad never being at home, and then he looked very said and I wanted to hug him and say, "It doesn't matter," but I wasn't brave enough.

I went home soon after that and found my supper on a plate and a note which read, WE WAITED AND WAITED FOR YOU. WE WANTED YOU TO COME WITH US. MUM. And I didn't even wonder where they had gone, because I was still thinking about Josh and about Fantasy.

Jenny collected a pile of recent Horse Sale catalogues, if that's the right word, and went through them. But there wasn't a lop-eared horse in any of them but then as Mark said disparagingly, no one would advertise his ears anyway.

The little ponies were making great progress; they had been wormed and deloused, and watched over like invalids, and they loved every moment of it. We called the roan Rowan, and the bay with the star predictably Star and Gillian named the palomino Goldie and Sarah the other bay Prince.

On the Saturday following the disastrous visit to Prospect House, we helped at the jumble sale. Josh and I served teas at 30p a time. People fought over the jumble which was made up of mounds and mounds of second-hand clothes, some quite decent, others old and smelly. And the bric-a-brac stall made £150. Jenny ran the raffle and a lady called Mrs Armstrong won the first prize which was a bottle of champagne. A child won a box of scented soap, and a man won a pair of tights which made everyone laugh. Then Jenny made a speech thanking everyone for coming; she explained our aims and our hopes for the future; she finished by saying that if anyone saw a black horse with flopping ears please would they let us know.

On Sunday the telephone rang. Jenny and Mark

were out. Josh was schooling Trooper in the covered school, so I answered it. A voice asked for the manager of Horsehaven. I didn't know what to say because we had no manager, so I offered to take a message and the voice said, "I've read a lot about you and to cut a long story short, my husband died a few weeks back and I'm left with his Land Rover, which I hate, and I'm wondering whether you would like it. You see it was his pride and joy and I know he would want it to have a good home. What do you think?"

I remembered Mark kicking his car and doubted whether we would be a good home; but then I thought, Land Rovers aren't like horses Cathy, they're just machines, so who cares?"

"Yes please, we would love it," I said then. "We are almost without transport, so it would be absolutely fantastic." But my voice must have sounded too enthusiastic, or too young, because after that she asked to speak to the manager again.

Saying, "Hang on please," I rushed to the covered school and screamed, "Get off Josh. You've got to be the manager. We're going to be given a Land Rover. Hurry."

"But I'm not the manager," protested Josh, dismounting.

"Just say you are," I cried snatching Trooper, mounting and riding him round the covered school. And I thought, brilliant, a Land Rover! It's just what we want and everything started to feel better and Trooper's stride was long and calm beneath me and I thought if only one could ride for ever and ever, and never stop.

Josh talked for ages. When he returned he said, "She's going to bring it over tomorrow morning, and she wants Mark or Jenny to run her back."

"Did you say you were the manager?" I asked dismounting.

"No, I said I was the stud groom," replied Josh laughing.

Later Gillian rang to say that the jumble sale had made £220.05p, and everything seemed to be getting better and better except that we would probably never see Fantasy again.

After that Josh and I took hay out to the fields, and Josh said that Trooper must have been really well schooled once, and needed a home where he was only ridden occasionally. I said that I didn't want him homed, that I never wanted anything homed again.

Gradually it grew dark. We were mounting our bikes to go home when Mark and Jenny returned. Leaping off I shrieked "Good news," and Josh said, "We're being given a Land Rover. It's arriving tomorrow." And then interrupting each other constantly, we told them about the telephone call, and having had several drinks they danced about the yard together, and Jenny cried, "Our luck is changing, hurray," and Mark said, "I'm sure you're right. Or am I dreaming? A Land Rover!" And then they both asked a lot of questions we couldn't answer, before we rode away together on our bikes, our heads suddenly light with relief, because now with luck we would never have to ride in Bill's truck again.

That night there was a frost and when I woke in the morning everything outside was tinselled silver. I lay in bed thinking about Fantasy and then I thought that Samantha would soon be home from school and would spoil everything. I thought, she'll follow Josh around all day long, and she'll keep giving Jenny money, so buying her love. She'll stand and criticise and be Lady Muck and no one will say anything, because of her generosity. And now I hated my small room and the boring old street lamp outside the window. And I thought Mum's right when she says, "Money speaks." I saw Samantha's hands clean when mine were dirty, her clothes perfect when mine were worn, and I thought Josh will prefer her to me, and that was almost as bad as Fantasy disappearing.

But by next Saturday my gloom had lifted. I found Mark and Bill painting the stable doors ready for the Open Day, Josh was installing his computer in the small room next to mine which was to be the office. Gillian and Sarah were chattering to one another as they groomed Squid and Fidget. Rowan gave me a special whinny. She was beginning to look pretty with a coat the colour of red squirrel and a silver grey mane. Jenny said that Flora Duckett must have bought the ponies as foals. and that her intentions had been good. But otherwise, Jenny remained glum, still blaming herself for letting Fantasy go too easily to an unknown fate.

Later that day an elderly couple appeared in the yard. The man was tall, with long legs in riding boots and wearing a Barbour. The woman wore a skirt, sheepskin boots and a sheepskin coat.

"Is this Horsehaven?" they asked Josh who smilingly directed them to the office where Jenny was trying out the computer. Jenny emerged and watched them shake hands and heard the man say, "My name is Hugh Chamberlain. To cut a long story short, my old mare died last night, and my other horse is crazy with grief. He doesn't work any more. I hung up my boots ten years ago, so I need a companion as soon as possible." And all the time he was looking round the yard with a horseman's eye.

"We do need references," replied Jenny warily.

"No problem, you can have my vet's and a host of others."

"We'll need to look at your place first," said Josh in a determined voice.

"You're welcome; there's a big shelter in the park, and plenty of stabling if it turns really cold."

"And he'll be spoilt rotten," said his companion whom I decided must be Mrs Chamberlain.

Jenny showed him Trooper, then she told him about Queenie until he exclaimed, "Not Ron's old pony! Oh the brute. She made his name you know. Oh what a cad! I'd like to see her straightaway if you don't mind."

"She's covered with mud," said Jenny.

"I don't mind that..." We followed Jenny like a line of ducks following their leader. Queenie whinnied. Hugh Chamberlain talked to her for a long time calling her all sorts of affectionate names like, "My little old lady," and "The Maltese Cat," after the polo pony Kipling immortalised. Then he said, "Tell you what, jump into my vehicle and come and see my place. I insist on it. Come on. All of you, just pile in." Remembering our last trip, Sarah and Gillian decided to stay behind. Josh and I, feeling grand, sat in the back with

Mrs Chamberlain.

"Actually hubby's famous," she said patting my arm as we drove away.

Not knowing what to say, I nodded in reply, then said, "Wow! That's great," and lapsed into silence.

Before long we arrived at an ancient house with many high chimneys surrounded by park land. An old dark brown horse was standing mournfully under a tree. He had a beautiful head, the sort you see in old paintings, and a wonderful long sloping shoulder.

"You see why he needs a companion," said Hugh Chamberlain stopping the Range Rover. "Poor old chap, his heart's breaking."

Josh and I talked to the old hunter who was called Duke, while a trailer was hitched to the Range Rover, bedded with straw and loaded with rugs, bandages, a tail guard, a haynet of hay and a beautiful headcollar. We did not stay long for it was obviously a perfect home.

On the way back Jenny said, "There's just one problem, Hugh. Queenie was supposed to go for meat to settle Ron's account.

"No hassle. How much is it? 300? Fine," replied Hugh Chamberlain smiling at Jenny. And now it seemed more like a sale than a loan, but then I knew Queenie would have been sold anyway if she had gone for meat, and this was infinitely better than going to an abattoir.

"Hubby's very generous. He's always raising money for charity," purred Mrs Chamberlain.

I thought of Queenie in the park. We would miss

her of course, but that didn't matter, what mattered was that Ron's account would be settled at last and Queenie would be happy.

Getting out of the Range Rover I explained that among the polo ponies Queenie had always been bottom of the pecking order.

"There won't be a pecking order with Duke. He's a gentleman; they'll talk about old times together. I'm so happy I came to see you today; watching Duke mourn was breaking my heart," said Hugh.

"It was really. You should have seen him. You couldn't even eat breakfast, could you my dear?" asked his wife.

And so it came about that Queenie left us, swathed in leg bandages, wearing a tail guard and a rug, and a headcollar with brass buckles on it. As she left, the other polo ponies neighed in a half hearted way, then shook their heads and returned to grazing.

"She was always the odd one out," said Josh.

"I shall miss her," I answered.

"Same here, but it's for the best," Jenny replied.

And so soon the hay barn was filled with hay again and Bill and Mark started painting the stable doors ready for our first ever Open Day. The Land Rover was parked by the house and every time we saw it I knew that miracles do happen. Hugh Chamberlain rang to say that Queenie had settled in really well and Duke had taken on a new lease of life, and I couldn't help thinking how different it might have been if Fantasy had found such a home. The little ponies were turned out now only coming in at night, to be stuffed with extra vitamins.

I started biking to Horsehaven after school and often Josh did too. There never seemed enough time for all the things I wanted to do. When I fell into bed at night it was to sleep the sleep of total exhaustion. My parents were worried about my homework and terrified by my biking home after dark, so late sometimes that the shops were shut and the pubs opening, but Horsehaven had now taken over my life. I ignored taunts at school, ignored the boys who wanted dates, or a kiss behind the sports pavilion. I ignored the discussions on clothes and make-up which went on all the time among the other girls in my class. I refused all invitations to parties. Horsehaven became my armour against the world, as long as I was there and could be part of it, none of the rest mattered. There was little time left for food. Mum gave me sandwiches to take to school. Dad gave me lectures about the difficulty of finding employment without educational qualifications, and he certainly knew about it, being unemployed himself. But I was deaf to all of it. At night I dreamed of Horsehaven, at school my mind wandered there and would not return to lessons. Only when I thought about Fantasy was I miserable; the rest of the time I was happier than I had ever been.

And because of that my whole appearance improved. Spots vanished from my face. I grew slim. And then the holidays arrived. School broke up for Christmas and Sammy reappeared. Recently I had not thought too much about Josh. Looking back he seemed always with me - feeding, mucking out, pushing wheelbarrows through mud. If a bale was too heavy to lift he was there to help. He mended punctures on my bike, tightened the brakes. He was simply part of my love affair with Horsehaven, and as it turned out, a larger part than I ever imagined.

CHAPTER TEN

OUR FIRST OPEN DAY

We plaited most of the inmates of Horsehaven for our first Open Day, groomed them until there wasn't a speck of mud on their long winter coats, stabled them, oiled their hoofs. Now looking back I realise that our plaits were probably too thick and too few. And however hard we tried the little ponies remained thin with poor misshapen hoofs. But Squid and Fidget looked fantastic and even Trooper appeared less like a wrung out dishcloth. Mrs Sykes was a pain. Arriving early, she was furious to find the covered school full of stalls selling things. She told me that none of us bothered about Romance any more and asked why his hoofs weren't oiled. Josh calmed her down calling her his Mrs S, fetching the tin of oil and oiling Romance's hoofs himself, saying, "There you are mrs S," patting her on the shoulder, adding "All done in a trice - no problem."

Secret and Mystery now had their owners' name painted above their own on their loose-box doors. Because Barney Banks was opening the fete they would be the stars and Jenny had groomed them for ages. The press were expected to show up and Barney's publicity agent. At half past one the first cars started to arrive. Bill was organising the parking and Mark as usual taking the money. Josh and I were wearing ties. Jenny had lent me a riding coat. Stuck on a tree by the entrance to the stables was a notice which read: HAVE YOU SEEN THIS HORSE? with a photograph and description of Fantasy underneath. Jenny had marshalled half a dozen friends to run the stalls in the covered school. Mark's mother had come to serve teas. I could not believe that it was really happening, that we were at last a proper Sanctuary; it made me realise that almost anything is possible if you want it badly enough and that the saying, 'faith can move mountains' may be true.

People kept coming, more and more of them. Most of them asked the same question. "Where's Barney Banks?" His fame had never impressed us before. His horses had seemed more important, and we had treated him just like everyone else. Looking back on that first Open Day there wasn't a lot to see. Later our Open Days would be really professional, This one lacked something in spite of all our efforts. There were no notices to stop people feeding the ponies. so Squid and Fidget ate and ate until Fidget bit a small child's finger. and Squid started putting his ears back and demanding titbits in a bullying way. Mrs Sykes watched it all with a critical eye. It wasn't long before she was standing in front of Romance's box saying, "I'll have you know this horse isn't a rescued animal. He cost me £3,000. He's a dressage horse."

The little ponies grew bolder and presently stuck their noses over their loose-box doors - they were too small to look over properly - while Trooper hating the intrusion turned his back on the visitors. I thought then that every horse is different, just as we are different. I thought that I would like to study the minds of horses when I left school, become the Anthony Clare of the horse world, and then I thought I would never get anywhere in life because I was slipping back at school all the time and without education there would be no hope.

And then Sammy appeared with a boy she introduced as Vince. His hair was short and he wore one earring. Sammy smiled at me before hurrying across the yard to talk to Josh.

A minute later Barney Banks arrived in a Rolls Royce with a chauffeur. Someone set up a microphone. Then Barney Banks made an effusive speech; he spoke about horses going for slaughter, of long journeys in sealed containers; of ponies travelling with broken legs, of old horses dying on ships. He spoke of beloved animals being sold unthinkingly to bad homes, and all the time I kept remembering Fantasy and how he had welcomed me in the early mornings and of his absurd lop ears. Barney Banks talked of foals shipped via Ireland to become parts of sausages, and he said that was why Horsehaven had come into being; solely because of the cruelty of man to horses, ponies and donkeys, who were the most tortured and exploited animals in the world. And then a screen was set up and we saw these poor distressed animals on film and by this time most of us were weeping. Finally he asked for donations for Horsehaven. It was a great performance and when he sat down there was prolonged clapping before a crowd surged forward begging for autographs. And Barney, seeing that no one was giving donations, asked for a pound each time he signed his name.

Sammy watched him with shining eyes and kept saying over and over again, "I rode with him. I did really." Cameras were out now and video cameras too. Mark made an announcement telling everyone that there were teas and stalls in the covered school. And Jenny asked that the ponies should not be fed titbits. Looking at her I knew that everything had been worthwhile because it was obvious that our first Open Day was a colossal success.

At the end of the day there was a lot of handshaking and a lot of promises given. Sammy followed Josh around, helping him change rugs, promising to come every day throughout the Christmas holidays, which made my heart sink right down to the bottom of my muddy boots. Even Mark was smiling. Pulling at his one ear-ring with discontentment etched on his ugly face, Vince watched Sammy. "I don't know what she sees in this place," he said glumly.

I looked at him. His shoulders were broad, his legs short, his neck thick. He was a bulldog, whereas Josh was a pale golden retriever, and Sammy like me preferred the retriever.

"Coming here is a change from home - a reason for being alive," I suggested.

"It's more likely she sees something in Josh. Yes, that's what it is - she fancies him," said Vince.

I knew he had hit the nail on the head and felt empty inside.

"What about us being mates, nothing serious; you know what I mean," asked Vince.

"There's no time," I said vaguely picking up a fork. "I'm just too busy for relationships."

At last the work was done. Jenny told us that there was still no news of Fantasy. "I think you must accept the unacceptable," she said.

"That he's dead?" I asked.

"So what?" asked Vince. "You've got plenty more of them, too many if you ask me, it's not as though he was your only horse, is it?"

The remark made him a leper in our midst. "But we loved him," I said slowly. Of course Vince could not understand. To him horses were like bicycles - replaceable.

"No arguing. Go home. Scram. Can't you see it's dark?" asked Jenny. Josh and Sammy both had mountain bikes and left together. Vince followed them on foot.

When I reached home Mum was waiting for me - a worried hen waiting for her only chick to return. "I thought something had happened to you," she said. Dad was watching television in the sitting room.

"You must stop worrying. I'm quite old," I told her shutting the door after me.

"But such terrible things happen," she said filling the kettle. "I think Dad has a job at last. It's not definite yet, but we'll know for sure after Christmas," she continued switching on the kettle.

I heard Mum talking, but at that moment her words

didn't really register, because I was still seeing Sammy and Josh leaving Horsehaven together and the empty feeling was back in my stomach.

"Your Dad's really excited," continued Mum. "Chuffed, that's what he is."

"I'm so pleased for him," I answered imagining Dad dressed in some sort of uniform delivering things, or wielding a shovel, or maybe reading gas meters. Mum went on talking, but now I wasn't really listening. I was thinking that Sammy would be following Josh around for the next three weeks or, worse still, if she left her boarding school, every weekend as well.

"It's some way away, we have to move," Mum continued. But now I was thinking of Christmas. I hadn't much money, but I must give Josh a present, and Mum and Dad would expect something too, and what about Jenny? I thought.

"Anyway we'll soon be out of debt when Dad starts working again," said Mum cheerfully. "You'll be able to have proper pocket money then, until you get a job that is."

CHAPTER ELEVEN

CHRISTMAS

I bought a paperback for Josh; hand cream and scented soap for Mum and a modern corkscrew for Dad. I bought a box of cards and sent them to everyone else I knew including Jenny, Mark, Bill and all the helpers at Horsehaven. I hoped and prayed that these people would not give me presents.

Three days before Christmas we took Squid and Fidget into Cowford. Jenny had been to see the police first so that we wouldn't be accused of anything awful like begging. We unboxed them in the supermarket car park. We had just put frills of red paper round their necks and red ribbons on their tails. They looked amazed by everything they saw and with heads high and ears pricked forward, they really did look sweet.

Samantha had gone to London to see CATS. She had wanted Josh to go with her, but he hates London and isn't into musicals, so Vince went instead. (It seemed that Sammy was becoming the sort of girl who couldn't go anywhere without a boy in tow.)

Josh and I stood with little piebald Fidget outside

the town hall, which had a huge Christmas tree lit up nearby, and a Father Christmas inside. It was a perfect place for collecting money. Poor Father Christmas, I'm sure we bagged lots of his trade, for as soon as people saw Fidget they surged forward to put money in our collecting box which had HORSEHAVEN written on it in bold red letters. One woman pushed in a ten pound note; small children were lifted up to put money in; old people hobbled across the market square to say that they must give us something, however little. No one wanted to know for whom we were collecting. The sight of Fidget was enough! After an hour we grew cold and took it in turns to walk round the square. Then Josh suggested we try a pub and we took Fidget into one called the Three Tuns, which had a low ceiling and a tiny bar. We were brought cider and Fidget was offered beer and soon our collecting tin was full to overflowing. Jenny, Sarah and Gillian had done equally well by the supermarket. When we rejoined them the street lights were coming on; people were going home for tea, carol singers were singing The First Noel. Suddenly I wanted to cry with happiness.

Loading the ponies I said, "Is it all right if I come and give the horses special breakfasts on Christmas morning Jenny?"

Jenny said that would be fine, but I mustn't stay too long, because Christmas was a family occasion and I should be at home. Josh said that his mother would be working a night shift and wouldn't be awake till midday, so he would do the same.

After we had settled the horses, we counted the

money we had collected and it came to £209.08p. Sarah and Gillian went home. Jenny, Josh and I sat drinking tea in the kitchen and it was fantastic to be on our own again, just the three of us.

"If only Fantasy was here everything would be perfect," I said.

"We can't always get everything right all the time, no one can," replied Jenny.

"And he may be all right living in a lovely loose-box being spoilt rotten," suggested Josh.

"So stop worrying Cathy. You're such a pessimist," added Jenny.

"Her mother's a worrier too," said Josh.

Jenny told us that Bill was coming on Christmas Day to help. "He's joining us for our Christmas dinner, he had nowhere else to go," she said.

"Poor Bill," said Josh. "Sammy asked me to go over to her place, but I'm not going, because I can't stand her parents; her father's so rich and her Mum is into clothes and furnishings, and the house is just like a furniture show room inside. Her Mum can't bear you to touch a wall because you might leave a finger mark behind. It makes me sick."

Hardly knowing why," I said "I bet her bedroom's different. I bet it's full of horsey things."

"I've never been allowed upstairs, so I wouldn't know," replied Josh smoothly. "But I did help her pull up all the dead ragwort in the field, not that she did much."

I felt gloomy now. I imagined Josh and Sammy pulling up ragwort together. They must have become real friends by this time.

We washed our mugs at the sink. Tomorrow was Christmas Eve but suddenly it didn't feel like it.

"I'm off then," I said.

"Take care," said Jenny.

"I'll catch you up," added Josh. But he never did. In all the gardens on the way home and in many windows Christmas trees shone bright. The sounds of carols echoed along a dark, empty street. Coloured lights lit up the forecourts of pubs. Shop windows were decorated. I wished I was grown up. I wanted Josh to like me, not Sammy.

When I reached home Mum was icing the Christmas cake. "How did it go? Did you make a lot?" she asked.

"Yeah, over £200."

"But that's wonderful, well done!" she said. "But why so downcast?"

"It's nothing. Everything's fine."

On the night before Christmas I dreamt that Josh and Sammy had run away together. "Good luck to them," exclaimed Jenny laughing. Next I was on a beach where I found a dead horse washed up - Fantasy! I knelt down and looked into his eyes, but there was no life in them and his absurd ears were covered with sand; and suddenly there was sand everywhere and the sea was coming in and there was no escape. I woke then to find a full stocking on the bottom of my bed full of lovely presents. I dressed, crept downstairs and took them out in the kitchen.

I had prepared sliced carrots in the kitchen the night before and now I put them in a plastic bag. Then I slipped outside and set off for Horsehaven on my bike.

The town was silent; only a few cats were stealing along the streets like phantoms. The last bit of road was covered with the carnage of the night before - a squashed rabbit, a dead magpie, a rat, someone's beloved dog; all long past reviving. I tried not to look.

I was the first to arrive at Horsehaven. At the sound of my bike, sleepy heads appeared over loose-box doors. "Merry Christmas" I shouted dismounting. I loved being first because then everything seemed to belong to me. I mixed feed, added my sliced carrots. Trooper pushed me affectionately. The ponies neighed. Romance blew down his nose at me. I missed Fantasy. Squid and Fidget nearly knocked me over when I delivered their buckets of breakfast. And now the polo ponies were milling around in the mud by their field gate, while Secret banged on his door wanting me to hurry, and Mystery whirled round and round his loose-box and then stood digging up his bed. Drizzle dropped from a sky which was still dark in places, though dawn was already breaking in the East.

When everyone was fed, I stood looking at Rowan and I thought that she really was a very pretty pony, almost a show pony, and because of that, would be easy to rehome. Then I wished that the polo ponies could be stabled, because they looked like poor relations covered with mud in their field; but Ron had forbidden it. He wanted them to be tough he said, and for this reason rugs were forbidden too. Then I realised I had forgotten to feed Romance and had to check the blackboard in the tack room to make sure that I added the right vitamins to his feed. He watched me anxiously and nearly knocked me over as I went into his loose-box.

Now the lights were coming on in Jenny's house. Then smoke emerged from a chimney; next she opened the back door to call, "Is that you Cathy? You're early. Come inside. Happy Christmas."

"Happy Christmas," I called back.

Once inside she handed me a small package which contained yellow riding gloves, the sort I had been wanting for ages. Soon after that Sammy arrived closely followed by Josh. I gave Josh his present; he gave me mine which was a black china horse for my collection. "In memory of Fantasy," he said. It was light now. I thanked Josh and then Sammy gave him an expensive silk tie and Jenny and me silk scarves. As she did so she said to me, "Don't worry that you could only manage a card; we can't choose our parents. And I'm just plain lucky."

I went red and didn't know how to answer. Josh said quickly, "I'm not very lucky either, because Dad isn't home, though we are expecting him for the New Year."

"Well I'm having a party and you are all invited, and you've got to come, I order you. But most of all, you Josh, wearing your silk tie of course," said Sammy laughing.

"What about Vince?" I asked.

"Who's Vince? Oh him, yes, him too I suppose," replied Sammy. "If he's still around that is."

"What about the feeding?" asked Josh.

"All done," I said. "Even Romance."

I was about to go home when Bill turned up. "Thank goodness you are still here, I've brought you a present Cathy," he cried, climbing out of his truck.

"Me? Why me?"

"Because you're my honorary grand-daughter," he said. "And you just wait till you see what I've bought you.

Slowly I opened the enormous parcel. Inside was a new Barbour. "Now you will be as good as nibs," he said.

"Who's nibs?" I asked flustered by being given so much.

"Sammy of course." (Fortunately Sammy and Josh had gone home by this time.)

I put on the coat, looking at myself in the mirror in the covered school. Bill was smirking. "All you need now is a pair of green wellies," he said.

I thanked him again and again, but truth to tell I didn't feel right in the Barbour, it wasn't me, not really. I would have looked all right in a cheaper waxed jacket, but not in a Barbour. It simply wasn't right for the street where I lived. To do it justice I needed a Range Rover.

"Wear it home. Just see what your Mum says when she sees you in it," beamed Bill.

I thanked Bill again and told him it was far too expensive, but he said that he hadn't a single grandchild, and that he had been doing a few odd jobs for people so wasn't short of a bob or two.

The best of Christmas seemed over now. When I arrived home, Mum and Dad were waiting for me with hurt faces. "We thought you were never coming back," Mum said sadly and then her mouth fell open when she saw the Barbour and she cried, "Whoever gave you that?"

I found it difficult to explain. They didn't like the idea of Bill adopting me as a grandchild and they saw the coat as a slur on them. But at last we got to the Christmas tree and to opening our presents with cries of gratitude and glee. But Mum's and Dad's present of a video of the Spanish Horses of Vienna was overshadowed by the barbour and I could see that they were upset, and I didn't know how to put it right. Christmas dinner was too much as usual. I was becoming a veggie so I didn't appreciate the turkey which didn't help. Afterwards we watched television and I fell asleep and dreamt that Sammy and Josh were kissing in the hay barn. Josh saw me and called out, "Go away, you horrible peeping Tom."

We ate the Christmas cake for tea. I praised it to the skies, but Mum was still put out. "Bill's made it seem as though we couldn't give you anything nice," she said.

"Inadequate like," added Dad.

"He didn't mean it like that. He's just a very generous person, that's all," I said.

"You shouldn't have accepted it," said Dad.

I longed to go back to Horsehaven, but that would have hurt them even more.

"Sit down girl," Dad said. "It's Christmas."

But my mind was spinning, my imagination running wild. I kept hearing Sammy's condescending remark again and again about not being able to choose my parents, and Josh's remark which followed. I wondered whether they had gone home together, for I hadn't seem them leave. I resolved to talk to Jenny about them. She would surely know how they felt for one another.

I put the china horse Josh had given me on my dressing table. I hung my Barbour on my door and put the yellow gloves in one of it's many pockets. I would keep them for best, I decided, for the next Open Day; for Sammy's New Year's party over some leggings and my long polo neck. Christmas was over now; but a new year was about to begin. And now suddenly I was filled with hope. I saw more and more horses and ponies arriving at Horsehaven, its fame spreading. I saw myself becoming Jenny's personal assistant, earning real money at last. I saw Josh growing bored with Sammy. Christmas was over but anything might happen in the New Year - it was wide open.

CHAPTER TWELVE

A HORSE BETWEEN MOTORWAYS

Mum kept mentioning Dad's new job. If I had been more in tune with her, I would have realised that she was trying to tell me something. But I had other things on my mind - Sammy and Josh; Trooper's arthritis; Mrs Sykes' complaints that none of us had time for Romance any more. Then there was Bill wanting me to wear my Barbour all the time, insisting that it was never meant only for best. Mark had a new job, which meant Jenny needed more help. And then we all got colds and went about talking in croaky voices. Gillian's and Sarah's became tonsillitis and they stayed away. The wind blew freezing cold from the East upsetting wheelbarrows, blowing hay out of our arms, making the horses nervous. It slammed doors behind you and blew down tools; it whistled down chimneys and rattled windows. At times it was like a demon let loose in the yard.

The first snow appeared, stinging our eyes, wet cold snow, which would suddenly obscure the sky, racing across the fields, great blankets of it. In spite of what Ron said we brought the polo ponies in, which meant more mucking out, but saved us from pushing wheelbarrows of hay through sudden gusts of freezing snow.

All through this, Sammy kept on about her party. She had invited fifty guests she said, but now feared that many would not make it. Josh and I were too tired to think about it. Jenny had a throat infection and was on antibiotics. I wore my Barbour now, it had become my main defence against the elements. And then on New Year's Eve just when we were winding ourselves up for Sammy's party, a man rang Jenny.

It was half past three exactly when he rang; I know, because I looked at my watch as Jenny came running from the house croaking, "Action stations. We're in business. Pony nuts, a headcollar, torch, a rug and hurry." Josh and I ran to get things together, our hearts hammering, while Jenny hitched the trailer to the Land Rover. Another minute and we were inside.

"Why? Where? What for?" asked Josh.

"I'll tell you as we go. Get the map handy Josh." Jenny's small hands were tight on the steering wheel now, her face bright with fever.

"There's a horse in a small field between three motorways, hang on a minute and I will give you the road numbers Josh. Boys have been stoning him. And there's no sign of food or shelter or even water. The police are there. Got it?" asked Jenny.

of the Land Rover. I thought of Sammy and her party. We would never make it now I thought, not with a dying horse on our hands.

"Give me the road numbers," Josh said. He put on an inside light and studied a map.

"Who rang?" I asked.

"The man who called the police. He was afraid the RSPCA might put the horse down straight away, so he must be in bad shape," replied Jenny.

Sleet lashed the Land Rover. I thought of a horse dying in a field between motorways - alone.

"Left here Jenny, then left at the next roundabout. I hope I'm getting it right, it's a hell of a place to find," Josh said.

It was warm in the Land Rover and I must have fallen asleep, because the next thing I heard was Josh crying, "Oh help, we're going the wrong way on the motorway and there isn't an exit for five miles at least."

"Oh how could you?" cried Jenny. "You idiot. You absolute idiot." And it was snowing again.

"At this rate the horse will be dead by the time we get there," I said.

"Shut up Cathy, just shut up," shouted Jenny.

Visibility was growing less all the time. The windscreen wipers were working non stop. I thanked God that we weren't in Bill's truck or worse, in Mark's old car. We hadn't packed any provisions, not even a rug to keep us warm if we were snowbound, only a horse rug.

"Oh how I hate people," cried Jenny, driving down an exit road, over a bridge back the other way.

Josh was so tense now that sitting beside me he felt like a bomb ready to go off. He was trying to read the map with help from the motorway lights.

It was half past four but it seemed like night already. "Left at the next roundabout. all right?" asked Josh in a tight voice. "Then right at the next one, then right again and we should be there."

I saw the police car first, hazard lights flashing. Jenny slowed down, her face relaxed for the first time since leaving Horsehaven. Slowly she parked the Land Rover and trailer.

"I don't know whether he's worth rescuing madam," a police officer greeted us. "I felt tempted to put him down myself, if I had had a gun that is."

We climbed a broken, padlocked gate. There was no shelter, just wire fences, broken tins, bits of old cars rusting away. The police officer shone a powerful torch on the miserable field saying, "Mind as you go. Watch it now. He's over there in the corner."

For a moment I thought of Sammy making canapes, her mother, who wouldn't have her walls touched, helping and her Dad opening bottles. It seemed a world away.

Then we were looking down at an exhausted horse wearing a tattered waterproof rug, which had rubbed him raw in places. Jenny was talking to him, holding out food which he ignored, saying, "Come on old fellow, get up. Come on, try."

We knelt in the mud and the snow and massaged his legs. He raised his head a little and we saw that one of his eyes was closed completely and that his mane was sticky with blood.

"Did you catch the boys?" asked Jenny quietly.

"We've got their names and addresses," the police officer said.

"What will happen to them?" demanded Josh.

"Not much, they are only twelve."

"Their parents should be locked up," Jenny said in a voice which was growing croakier each passing minute. "Locked up and fined hundreds of pounds."

I put pony nuts under the horse's nose. His head was covered with mud and wet snow and then I saw something which made my blood run cold. "Look at him, Jenny," I cried. "Just look. He's got lop ears. It must be Fantasy!"

You can imagine how we felt then, how madly our hearts raced, while anger grew inside us like a storm about to break. We wiped the mud from the horse's face with our gloves and Jenny said, "Fantasy. Listen Fantasy. We've come to take you home."

"So get up Fantasy. Come on please," I pleaded.

I think at that moment we were all blinded by tears. Then with renewed vigour, we fell to massaging his legs again, and with freezing fingers I undid the buckles of his rug; the straps were covered with blood and hair and bits of skin; the surcingle was buckled as tight as it could go.

Now of course it was too bad for tears; sadness and horror were replaced by fury. Desperately we struggled to lift Fantasy, but he kept falling back into the snow. "We can lift him into the trailer, I know we can. We'll take down the partition, leave it here if necessary," croaked Jenny. So she and the others returned to the Land Rover and trailer while I stayed with

Fantasy. It was pitch black without the torch. I sat stroking his head while the others took down the gate, then drove towards us, lights blazing, tyres skidding.

Throwing down the ramp Jenny said in a determined voice, "Now come on Fantasy, up." Then she put the headcollar we had brought onto his poor head and she and I pulled on the rope while the police officer and Josh lifted his quarters, and slowly, oh how slowly Fantasy stood up. And oh what a pitiful sight he was then! "Why didn't someone do something before?" asked Josh accusingly.

"Going too fast to stop," replied the police officer matter of factly. "Someone's been feeding him on raw potato peelings and cooked cauliflower. Even I know that isn't good for horses."

Snow blew into our faces; the wind whipped us. Slowly we edged Fantasy to the ramp. Twice he stopped to cough, great heaving coughs which racked his whole body. Slowly, slowly we put his hoofs on the ramp, showed him the feed inside, rustled the straw bed. Slowly we heaved at his quarters.

"He's probably dehydrated too, there's no sign of water here. It was light when we found him, so I had a good look round. There will have to be a prosecution, there's no doubt about that," said the police officer.

"Walk on Fantasy, walk on," croaked Jenny.

I patted his poor thin neck and let him smell my hair. I rubbed his silly lop ears and stroked his dear familiar face. "You're going home, your box is waiting for you there," I told him.

He walked forward then, up the ramp and into the

trailer, while Jenny croaked, "Well done Cathy," before she and Josh threw up the ramp and fastened it.

Fantasy didn't smell like himself any more. He smelt of rotting vegetables and dirty wet horse rug. He helped himself to hay, then let it fall from his mouth uneaten.

"You can stay with him until we get on the road Cathy," croaked Jenny through the little door in the front of the trailer.

"Stop talking Jenny. Tell me what you want said in a whisper," commanded Josh.

The Land Rover wheels spun, the trailer wheels became bogged down. It took us nearly an hour to get out of that dreadful field.

"Worst New Year's Eve I can remember," said the police officer.

"Same here," agreed Josh.

I climbed out of the trailer.

"I'll put my lights on and show you the way," said the police officer.

"Well anyway we've found him. So we won't have to look any more," Josh said.

"And how!" croaked Jenny.

"How could it have happened?" I asked. "How could it?"

And Jenny croaked back, "I just don't know."

I don't remember much of the journey home. I think most of us remained deep in our own thoughts, though what mine were I can't recall. I remember Josh looking at his watch and saying, "We'll never make Sammy's party now," and I remember saying, "Are you upset?"

"Not really. She gets on my nerves," he said.

"But I thought you liked her."

"I do. She's fun, but you can have too much of her," Josh said. And then I felt a little warmer.

When we reached home we bedded down Fantasy's old box and fetched him water and took off the terrible rug and bathed his wounds. Every bone in his body seemed visible. His long back made him look worse than he would otherwise have done. Jenny bathed his shut eye. We brushed him gently before putting on a new, clean rug, leaving it unbuckled at the front. Jenny made him a warm mash full of molasses, bran, boiled oats and cubes. She added sliced carrots and apples, her best dessert apples bought for Christmas.

In the kitchen Mark had left a note; it read, GONE TO SAMMY'S PARTY. SEE YOU THERE."

"I won't be going to the party and we won't call out a vet tonight because I don't want him to say the usual things, you know, 'he had a good innings,' 'it's best to put him out of his misery,' that sort of thing," croaked Jenny.

It was half past eight by this time. I could have gone to Sammy's party and been late, but at this moment I didn't feel up to it and deep down I had never wanted to go.

"I'll drive you both home," offered Jenny. "The weather's too bad to go on your bikes. I'll just unhitch the trailer first."

"And after that you had better go to bed, Jenny," suggested Josh.

"I hope Fantasy doesn't lose his eye," I said.

"We'll know when the vet's here in the morning,"

whispered Jenny.

Miraculously the snow had stopped. The sky had cleared. A moon shone down.

"I think I may get cleaned up and go to Sammy's party," said Josh. "If Mum will drive me that is."

I hardly heard him because I hated leaving Fantasy so much, but Jenny said that he would be all right now he was home.

"You'll watch over him won't you?" I asked.

"Of course."

"I shall feel so terrible if he's dead in the morning," I said.

"He won't be, I promise," Jenny said.

She dropped off Josh first. When we reached Cowford it was full of people shouting and singing. "You should go to the party. You never seem to go anywhere Cathy," croaked Jenny.

"I don't want to go anywhere," I said. "All I want to do is look after Fantasy. I don't want to go home either, Jenny; if you really want to know."

"Oh Cathy, that's an awful thing to say," said Jenny.

When we reached home, Jenny kissed me. "Happy New Year," she said. But before I got out of the Land Rover I asked what I had been wanting to for ages. "Do you think Josh likes me? I mean really? Or do you think he likes Sammy more, Jenny?"

"You of course, but you mean love don't you? And I should wait a bit for that. You are both too young. I know other people of your age think it's happening all the time, but mostly it's a mistake. Falling in love is very time-consuming and full of awful pitfalls, and you and Josh are both too young for a lasting commitment. Here endeth the first lesson," finished Jenny, her voice fading away to almost nothing. It wasn't much she had said, just a crumb when I had wanted a slice; but I knew in my heart she was right, for I was still only thirteen. Clambering down I said, "Thank you and a Happy New Year."

As I let myself in Mum called, "You're early. I thought you were going to a party."

"It's a long story. We've found Fantasy and he's alive, just."

And now I was home I felt broken up into little bits and so tired that I knew I would never survive Sammy's party even if I went.

"Well, I'm glad you're back early, because I want to have a talk with you, it's about Dad's job. I've been trying to tell you for weeks now. We'll be moving, there's a bungalow which goes with it, a mobile home really, with a little bit of garden; you'll be able to keep a dog - we've asked - you know you've always wanted one. And there's a riding school quite near, with lots of ponies. And they need helpers; we went there and looked. And there's a school quite near. And the sea's just down a path, just over the dunes really. Your Dad's got the job of looking after the caravan site, it's a lovely job, it really is. There were fifty applicants and he got it. We are so lucky. And we would have had to leave here anyway, because we're £1,000 behind with the mortgage." Mum was talking faster and faster; she was trying to see my face but I had turned away from her, because I was afraid that any minute I might begin crying. I felt guilty too, because I realised how worried she must have been about my reaction to the news, yet I couldn't stop myself crying out, "But what about Horsehaven?"

"You can come back and see how it is. We'll get a car; there may be one which goes with the job; only an old one of course, but they're mad keen to have your Dad, they really are. They are a lovely couple, not very old, but he's got high blood pressure. We clicked straight away, ever so nice they were." Now automatically Mum put the kettle on.

In a voice stifled by tears I asked, "How soon are you going?"

"Well, the job starts from the first, that's tomorrow, but we've said we'd be there by the seventh," Mum answered looking at me.

"The seventh? But that's only a week away," I cried.

Dad appeared then and putting his arms around me said, "You'll love it Cath; you'll get so brown, you won't know yourself; it's right by the sea, and there's lots to do. You can take up tennis, bowls, go dancing."

But I didn't want to take up tennis, play bowls or go dancing.

I only wanted one thing - to watch Fantasy get well and be at Horsehaven every spare moment of my life. There was nothing else I wanted, except maybe Josh to love me, and I knew that would never happen, because really whatever Jenny said, he was probably in love with Sammy by now. Another minute and I was running upstairs to my room, like a wounded animal to its lair.

I heard Mum say to Dad, "I knew she would take it badly. I've been trying to tell her for days now."

"She'll get over it. She'll love the sea," replied Dad

optimistically.

Next I heard Mum crying, and that made me feel worse than ever. I wanted to go downstairs and put my arms around her and say, "It doesn't matter Mum. I don't mind." But I couldn't, because I did mind, I minded more than I had ever minded about anything before in my entire life.

I put my recorder on to drown her voice and my own thoughts. It was so loud that Dad called up the stairs, "Put that thing off. Do you hear me?" But I didn't, because at that moment I didn't mind what anyone thought or said about me - it was irrelevant.

CHAPTER THIRTEEN

"WHAT'S THE MATTER?"

I was too upset to go down for supper so Mum left a tray outside my room with fish fingers and baked beans on it, and an apple. As I ate I kept seeing myself miles away on a caravan site, Fantasy getting better without me, Josh becoming more like a stranger than friend, a new school, myself trying to make friends all over again and failing. I wouldn't fit it. I knew it already - my voice was wrong, I was too tense and I didn't want a boyfriend, or only Josh.

It was snowing outside. It was New Year's Day but it didn't feel like it. Had Josh and Samantha danced all night? And kissed each other when the magic hour struck I wondered? I didn't sleep for hours. When at last I woke up, it was half past ten. I raced downstairs and found a note on the kitchen table which read: HAD TO GO OUT. BACK SOON. LOVE MUM AND DAD. I saw now that they had started to pack, for Mum's best wine glasses were neatly wrapped in tissue and put in a cardboard box, and her china plates were no longer on the dresser.

I ate cereals, bowl after bowlful and I didn't taste any of it. Then I turned the note over and wrote on the back, SORRY, C. I dressed and filled a bag with carrots and apples for Fantasy. I put on my Barbour and wellies and set off for Horsehaven on my trusty bike, already afraid of what I might find there.

I found Josh and Sammy mucking out, or rather Josh was, Sammy was watching. "Hi Cathy, what happened to you last night?" she called. "You missed a good party," said Josh pushing a wheelbarrow towards the muck heap.

Fantasy was looking over his box door. His neck looked pitifully thin; one eye was still shut. Seeing me with his good eye he whinnied.

"The vet's been," said Josh leaning on a fork. "He gave him shots of antibiotic. He's to be kept quiet and warm with lots to drink."

"And wormed in due course," added Samantha.

Fantasy was wearing a striped blanket under his rug, and flannel bandages on his legs. "What about his eye?" I asked.

"It's going to be all right," Sammy answered.

"So cheer up," said Josh. "You look like a dying duck in a thunderstorm."

Most of the work was done. I wished I hadn't overslept. I had wanted to be there when the vet came. I gave Fantasy the titbits I had brought; he took them gently examining each one with his good eye. "How did he go downhill so quickly? It's only about three months since he left here. The Mackintoshes must have been a bad home right from the start," I said.

119

"I expect they fought and ran out of money. Lots of people are like that," Josh answered. "They have such crazy ideas. Mum knew someone who bought three houses during the housing boom and then couldn't sell one of them for the same price - he killed himself."

"Charming," said Sammy smiling.

Josh put the tools away and came across to me and asked in a gentle voice, "For goodness sake Cathy, what's the matter?"

"She's just her usual self," said Sammy scathingly.

"Shut up. I know Cathy really well, you don't," snapped Josh.

"I can't tell you, not yet, later," I said.

"Is your mother dead? Your father? Come on speak out, you know the saying, 'a trouble shared is a trouble halved'." Josh was using the voice he used with horses, which would calm the wildest animal. But I wasn't a horse.

I looked round the yard and gulped. "I'm going to tell Jenny first. Is she better?"

"A bit. I'll come with you. I want to know what's the matter Cathy, because you're the heart and soul of this place, we all know that," continued Josh walking ahead of me towards the house. "You're going away aren't you? You've done something terrible haven't you? Your parents are breaking up, that's it, isn't it?" he asked.

"No, no, no," I shouted.

Jenny was typing a letter. "Oh it's you," she said. Her voice was clearer, almost back to normal.

"Cathy has something to say to you. She won't tell

me what it is, but it's obviously bad news," said Josh pushing me towards her.

I felt a real fool now. I looked at the floor which had mud on it and said, "I'm leaving, going away, all right?" and though I tried I couldn't keep my voice from shaking.

Jenny stopped typing.

"Dad's got a job looking after a caravan site. Our house hasn't been ours for ages. It belongs to a mortgage company," I explained miserably. "So we have to go anyway. I'm so sorry, but there it is. And when we started here, I promised to help and now I can't. I'm sorry," I finished.

"Well you don't have to feel guilty. It isn't your fault," said Jenny.

"What about school?" asked Josh.

"There's one just down the road and there's probably a job for me, and I can have a dog. They've done their best, but it still isn't here."

I went to the window and looked out. The yard was bathed in sunlight. Fantasy's head was hanging over his loose-box door. Mrs Sykes was tacking up Romance. I could see she was cross again. It was like so many other days had been, but because I was leaving everything seemed twice as beautiful. I thought of the wood when summer came deep in bluebells. I thought of Fantasy well again, sleek and round. I thought I'll never visit Queenie now. Never help train Rowan. It's over. It's going to be my past, not my future; it's finished.

"We must talk this through," said Jenny.

"She could live with us. I know Mum wouldn't mind,"

Josh suggested.

"She could stay here, be permanent. I need a helper, and she's got a room already," replied Jenny.

"But what will her parents say?" asked Josh. (They were talking about me as though I wasn't there.)

"We can sound them out. How much time have you got Cathy?" asked Jenny.

"Seven days, no six. Oh I don't know," I said.

Bill appeared then, his face creased in smiles. "And Happy New Year to you all," he cried cheerfully.

"Not for Cathy," said Josh.

"What's up then?" asked Bill.

I let the others do the talking. I went on looking out of the window saying goodbye to everything, to everything I loved.

Jenny explained my predicament. And now they were talking about me as though I wasn't there again, while I watched a disgruntled Sammy mount her bike and ride away, and Mrs Sykes run down her stirrups and tighten her girths before mounting Romance, and riding towards the covered school. Fantasy's head was still hanging over his loose-box door and I could see now that his injured eye was nearly open. And I thought all this will be nothing to do with me next week.

"We can do up the room, no problem. I've got a basin out in the back yard and plenty of paint, not to mention some hardboard for a wardrobe. It needs using if you know what I mean," said Bill. "It's only rotting away in my yard." (Bill always had everything one wanted in his back yard.)

"Tell you what, I'll nip over and fetch Cathy's parents right away. It'll only take a jiffy. Do you think they are at home Cathy?" he asked me.

"I expect so," I answered without turning round.

"I'll pay you as well. We can afford it. And now Mark's got such a good job, he can't help any more," Jenny told me, turning me round, saying, "Okay. Do you want to live here? Yes or no."

"Yes, if my parents don't mind. But they've asked about the area and there's a riding school nearby; but it could never be like here," I said. "And I don't particularly like the sea, or only on a horse, and I want to see Fantasy get better, and to visit Queenie and see if she's all right, and break in the ponies. There's just so much I want to do here," I said lamely.

"And I want you here," said Jenny.

"And so do I, because it just wouldn't be the same without you around," added Josh hugging me.

We looked at my room; it wasn't very big, just enough space for a bed, a chest of drawers, a bedside table and maybe a cupboard; but it would be my room and that's what counted.

Soon after that Bill drew up his truck and Mum and Dad stepped out. "So you want to stay here, is that it?" asked Dad in a slightly belligerent voice.

"Just come and look at the room," said Bill.

"She might be better here, than cycling all over the place in the dark. She might even get round to doing her homework," said Mum.

"I would see she did," said Jenny firmly. "I know what it's like to have no education. I mucked up my life that way. I wouldn't let Cathy make the same mistake."

Bill showed my parents the room, saying we could put a basin in the corner by the door and that there were plenty of electric points. "And I've got an electric fire she can have, and a lovely basin in my back yard; and with a spot of paint we could turn this room into a palace," he suggested pausing for breath.

Bridling, Mum said, "We have some furniture she can have you know, and a nice carpet for a start."

"Just the job," replied Bill unabashed.

I went outside. Josh followed me. "Well, do you really want to stay? Say something Cathy," he cried. "Tell them in no uncertain terms. Go on."

"Of course I do. What do you think?"

"Tell them, go on, tell them." Then grabbing my arm, Josh dragged me back to the house.

"Thank you very much, I definitely want to stay," I said. "Of course I shall visit you, Mum and Dad, because I shall miss you," I continued hugging them each in turn. "But I'll have a job here, and you know you've always wanted me to have one. And you won't have to worry about me getting home before dark any more."

"I'll bring her over to see you regular like in my truck," Bill said. "I'll sit on a bench and look out to sea. I might even hire a boat and do a bit of fishing, I would enjoy that. Then she could spend all day with you."

We plan to get a car ourselves," replied Mum coldly.

In the end, Dad stayed to help Bill decorate my room. Jenny took Mum home in the Land Rover. I followed on my bike.

I started to pack. Mum said, "I shall miss you. But

124

I'm sure it will be for the best. If that's what you really want."

"Yes I do, I really do," I said. "It may sound peculiar but it's all I want, there's nothing else except perhaps Josh to love me."

"You are too young to think like that," said Mum sharply.

Later I went back to Horsehaven. Fantasy's loosebox was bedded down with shavings. "He's got asthma," Josh explained, "caused by musty hay and living between motorways. Just think of the pollution." Fantasy looked tired but happy, like someone who has survived a long and terrible war, I thought.

"Are you happy now?" asked Josh looking at me.

"Yes but guilty too."

"Jenny says you're to have a day and a half off a week, if you like it or not, and there's a bus to Whitecliffe-on-Sea every Sunday all through the summer. So cheer up, you'll come back all brown, think of that," said Josh laughing.

Bill and Dad were laughing too. Fantasy was home, Josh and I were together almost holding hands; at that moment there was nothing else I wanted in the entire world; only for time to stand still.

But of course time doesn't stand still. Alerted by the police, a member of the RSPCA visited us and it was decided that Fantasy's owners should be prosecuted; so Jenny learnt what really happened when she went to Court to give evidence. Apparently Mrs Mackintosh had sold Fantasy to a builder called Simons for £800.

Mr Simon's wife was depressed, unemployed and had

always wanted a horse she could call her own. For good measure Mr Simons bought the dreadful field too, and a ton of hay and ten sacks of horse and pony cubes. He meant to put up a shelter for Fantasy before the cold weather came, but almost at once things started to go wrong. A customer failed to pay Mr Simons for a job he had done and suddenly he seemed to be facing bankruptcy. Mrs Simons found a job which entailed travelling all over Britain in a company car. She did not forget Fantasy; she found a teenager called Marion willing to feed him twice a day for a small sum of money. But Marion fell ill and soon had not the strength to push a wheelbarrow of feed half a mile to the field twice a day and as the evenings grew darker her parents grew increasingly worried and said she must stop.

In Court Marion insisted that she had called on Mr Simons and told him she could not go on; she had also left a letter addressed to Mrs Simons explaining the situation. But at the time he was arguing with a customer and it seems her words were forgotten almost as soon as they were spoken. As for the letter it simply vanished under a pile of papers and was never read.

So Fantasy remained unfed and without water for nearly a week, until we found him lying in the mud dying.

In Court the Simons's pleaded guilty and were fined £600 and banned from keeping a horse for six years. Mrs Mackintosh did not appear at all. Jenny said that we could prosecute her ourselves if we ever found her, but that the legal fees would be more than Horsehaven could bear. So much for justice.

"But I think we have learnt our lesson. Another time we will ask for references," Jenny said. "And Fantasy is going to get better. I feel it in my bones."

And he did, but it took a long time and a lot of care.

Read the second and third books in the
Horsehaven trilogy

HAVOC AT HORSEHAVEN

Adventures continue for Jenny, Josh and Cathy. More horses are rescued. Jenny is rushed to hospital; Cathy is left in charge. And then one night catastrophe strikes ...

HORSEHAVEN LIVES ON

Josh and Cathy are growing older but Horsehaven lives on. More horses and ponies are rescued and some are re-homed. A dear old lady, Alice, arrives to help and Horsehaven nearly has to close down but good fortune prevails in the end ...

Both available at £3.99